"So we have a deal, do we? We do things *my* way, no arguments, no more buts."

"Yes," she bit out.

"Good," John said, smiling wryly to himself at the thought that *yes* wasn't a word Scarlet was used to saying to men. But she was going to say it a lot during their time together. He would *make* her say it. No, he would make her *want* to say it.

For, that was what he craved all of a sudden. Not just Scarlet's compliance but her complete surrender.

All about the author...
Miranda Lee

MIRANDA LEE was born in Port Macquarie, a popular seaside town on the midnorth coast of New South Wales, Australia, and is the youngest of four children. Her father was a country schoolteacher and brilliant sportsman. Her mother was a talented dressmaker. When Miranda was ten, her father was transferred to Gosford, another coastal town in the countryside, much closer to Sydney.

After leaving her convent school, Miranda briefly studied the cello before moving to Sydney, where she embraced the emerging world of computers. Her career as a programmer ended after she married, had three daughters and bought a small acreage in a semirural community.

Following this, Miranda attempted greyhound training, as well as horse and goat breeding, but was left dissatisfied. She yearned to find a creative career from which she could earn money. When her sister suggested writing romances, it seemed like a good idea. She could do it at home, and it might even be fun!

It took a decade of trial and error before her first romance, *After the Affair,* was accepted and published. At that time, Miranda, her husband and her three daughters had moved back to the central coast, where they could enjoy the sun and the surf lifestyle once again.

Not long into her writing career, Miranda committed herself to writing a six-book series entitled *The Hearts of Fire,* with a deadline of just nine short months. Bravely, her husband left his executive position to stay home and support Miranda's writing career. He learned to cook and to clean, two invaluable household skills.

Numerous successful stories followed, each embodying Miranda's trademark style—pacy and sexy rhythms; passionate, real-life characters; and enduring, memorable story lines. She has one credo when writing romances—don't bore the reader! Millions of fans worldwide agree she never does.

Other titles by Miranda Lee available in eBook:

Harlequin Presents®

Miranda Lee

CONTRACT WITH CONSEQUENCES

HARLEQUIN®

entertain, enrich, inspire™

Recycling programs
for this product may
not exist in your area.

ISBN-13: 978-0-373-23853-8

CONTRACT WITH CONSEQUENCES

www.Harlequin.com

Printed in U.S.A.

CONTRACT WITH CONSEQUENCES

CHAPTER ONE

'DON'T you think you should start getting dressed?'

Scarlet glanced up from the Sunday paper which she'd been pretending to read for the last hour or so. She hadn't felt like talking, especially since the conversation always came round to the radical choice which Scarlet had made this year. Her mother had initially supported her decision to have a child on her own by artificial insemination, but lately she'd been expressing the opinion that it might not be such a good idea.

Scarlet needed negativity at the moment like a hole in the head!

Okay, so the procedure hadn't worked the first two times. That was not uncommon, she'd been told by the clinic. She just had to keep on trying and sooner or later she would conceive. It wasn't as though there was anything physically wrong with her, except perhaps that she was getting older. Which was why she'd decided to do this in the first place.

'What time is it?' she asked.

'Nearly noon,' her mother replied. 'We really should make an appearance at the Mitchells' no later than quarter-to-one. I know Carolyn's planning on serving lunch around one-thirty.'

Carolyn and Martin Mitchell had been their friends and neighbours for almost thirty years. They had two children: a boy, John, the same age as herself, and a girl, Melissa, who was four years younger. Over the years Scarlet had got to know the family well, though she liked some members more than others. Mr Mitchell had not long retired and today was their fortieth wedding anniversary, a milestone which Scarlet knew would sadly never figure in her own life.

Janet King's heart squeezed tight when she heard her daughter sigh. Poor love. She'd been so disappointed when her period had arrived this week. It was no wonder she didn't feel like going to a party.

'You don't have to go,' she said gently. 'I could make some excuse—say you're not feeling well.'

'No, no, Mum,' Scarlet said quite firmly, and stood up. 'I'm fine to go. Truly. Do me good.' And she hurried to her bedroom, thinking that it *would* do her good. She could have a few glasses of wine—now that she wasn't expecting. She also wouldn't have to spend the rest of the day defending her decision to have a baby on her own. Because no one—other than her mother—knew about her baby project. Frankly, she was sick and tired of her mum telling her how hard it was, bringing up a child on her own.

Admittedly, Janet King had first-hand knowledge of the subject, Scarlet's father having been killed in a car accident when Scarlet had been only nine. Scarlet knew full well how difficult life had been for her mother at that time, both emotionally and financially. Difficult for herself, as well. She'd adored her father and missed him terribly.

So, yes, she appreciated that raising a child without the support of a partner *would* be hard at times.

But not as hard as never having a child at all!

Just *thinking* about such a prospect made Scarlet feel physically ill.

She'd always wanted to be a mother, ever since she'd been a little girl. She'd grown up dreaming of one day falling in love with a wonderful man—someone like her darling dad—getting married and having a family of her own.

Scarlet had honestly believed it was only a matter of time after leaving school before that happened. Her plan had been to marry young so that she could enjoy her children. Never in her wildest dreams had she envisaged reaching the age of thirty-four still single and without her Mr Wonderful anywhere in sight.

But that was how her life had panned out. Sometimes, Scarlet simply couldn't believe it.

Shaking her head, she stripped off her dressing gown then turned her attention to the outfit which she'd already laid out on the bed earlier that morning—a purple woollen tunic dress, black silk polo underneath, black tights and black ankle boots. It didn't take her long to dress—she'd already showered and blow-dried her hair—after which she made her way along to the main bathroom to put her hair up and do her make-up.

Neither job took Scarlet all that long. At thirty-four, she had her grooming routine down pat.

The sight of the finished product in the large vanity mirror brought a puzzled frown to her forehead. Why, she wondered for the umpteenth time, had it come to this?

It wasn't as though she was an ugly girl. She was very attractive with a pretty face: cute nose, full lips, blonde hair and a good figure. Okay, so her breasts *were* on the smaller side, but she looked great in clothes, being tall and slender. On top of that she had a bright, outgoing personality. People liked her. *Men* liked her.

Despite that, she'd had a lot of trouble finding herself a steady boyfriend over the years. In hindsight, Scarlet now realised that her choice of career hadn't helped, but that hadn't occurred to her at the time. Not wanting to leave home and the Central Coast, she'd taken a hairdressing apprenticeship in the salon where her mother had worked, a move which had confounded a lot of people. She had, after all, achieved very high marks in her exams and could have pursued some high-flying profession such as communications or law, if she'd wanted to.

But becoming a journalist or a lawyer was not what Scarlet wanted out of life. She had other priorities which didn't include more years of studying and even more years clawing her way up the ladder to what some people thought of as success in life. At the same time, she did want an interesting job which she enjoyed.

Despite her teachers' warnings to the contrary, Scarlet had loved being a hairdresser, had loved the camaraderie with her co-workers and clients. Loved the feel-good feeling which came with completing a colour or a cut not just adequately but brilliantly. She soon gained a great reputation as a stylist and by twenty-five she and her mother had opened their own salon in a small shopping centre not far from Erina Fair. They would have preferred to locate their salon in Erina Fair—the shopping hub of the Central Coast—but the rents there were way too high.

Because of their loyal clientele, their business had still been a huge success.

But only on the financial front. Scarlet eventually had begun to see that being a hairdresser with mainly female clients was not conducive to meeting members of the opposite sex. Being an only child with no siblings wasn't an asset, either. Maybe if she'd had an older brother...

Not that she didn't try to meet men in other ways. For years she'd maintained a group of girlfriends from her school days and they went out regularly together to parties, clubs and pubs where, for some perverse reason, she would always be hit upon by the type of good-looking sleazebag who was only interested in one thing—though she didn't work this out till she'd been burned a few times.

One by one, she watched as her girlfriends found nice guys to marry—mostly through their more diverse careers or family connections. Scarlet had been a bridesmaid so many times, she began to dread weddings, not to mention the after-wedding parties where her married 'friends' always tried to hook her up with some guy who was usually drunk and was only there to have sex with at least one of the bridesmaids.

When the last of her unmarried girlfriends had found her future husband on an Internet dating site, Scarlet had tried that method, but it had been an unmitigated disaster. For some reason, she still seemed to attract the wrong type who only wanted the one thing.

Scarlet had never been a girl who liked sex for sex's sake. Not that she hadn't tried it a few times in her younger days; she had. But she had found the experiences so lacking in pleasure that by her twenty-first birthday she vowed to reserve giving her body till she really liked the guy she was with. Unfortunately, she'd really liked some of the good-looking sleazebags who'd successfully picked her up during her twenties. Even then, there'd been no bells and whistles going off for her in bed, leading Scarlet to the conclusion that maybe she needed to be deeply in love to enjoy sex. Either that, or she was seriously undersexed.

By the time she turned thirty, Scarlet had been so desperate to find someone to love—and who would love her in return—that she'd made the mammoth decision to change careers. She went to college at night, gained her real-estate licence then applied for a job at one of the Central Coast's largest and most successful agencies.

It had seemed a good move at the time. Suddenly, she was surrounded by lots of eligible young men who thought she was the best thing since they had built the freeway connecting the central coast to Sydney. She had admirers galore, one of whom stood out from all the rest. Jason was an estate agent at a rival agency and a coastie—like herself. A charming, extremely handsome guy who came from a local family and didn't try to get her into bed on their first date. Hallelujah! When they did finally go to bed, the sex, whilst not quite of the earth-moving variety, had been pleasurable enough for Scarlet to conclude she'd finally fallen in love, feelings which she assumed were mutual when Jason proposed to her on her thirty-second birthday.

Plans for their wedding were well underway when disaster struck.

It had been eighteen months ago, at their street Christmas party. Jason was unable to go with her, saying he had a work-related dinner at the Terrigal hotel which he was obliged to attend. She was showing everyone her engagement ring and having a wonderful time when John Mitchell—the party was at the Mitchells' house that year—took her aside and very quietly told her the most devastating piece of information.

Her first instinct was disbelief and denial. It couldn't possibly be true: her fiancé was not gay. He couldn't be!

It was the gentleness in John's voice—and the compassion in his eyes—which finally con-

vinced her he was speaking the truth. For it
wasn't like John Mitchell to be that nice to her.
Deeply distressed, she left the party straight
away, sending Jason a text that she had to see
him. She arranged to meet him at the park opposite the Terrigal hotel where she confronted
him with John's allegation. He initially denied
being gay, but she wouldn't let him lie to her
any more, and he finally admitted the truth. He
begged her not to tell anyone else, as he hadn't
fully accepted it himself, and she hadn't, but she
broke her engagement.

Christmas that year, therefore, was not very
happy. Neither was the New Year. Totally shattered, Scarlet resigned her real-estate job—she
couldn't bear to run into Jason all the time—and
went back to hairdressing where she hid herself
away for the whole year, her spirits very low.
She never told anyone the truth about Jason—
not even her mother—saying instead that she'd
found out he was cheating on her. Her girlfriends
were very sympathetic whilst encouraging her
to keep on dating. But she simply hadn't had the
courage to put herself out there again. She'd felt
like a fool, and a failure.

Scarlet had been quite relieved when John
Mitchell hadn't come home last Christmas. She
hated the thought of his looking at her with pity

again, or saying something crass like 'I told you so'. Apparently, he'd broken a leg climbing up some stupid mountain in South America and was unable to travel. She was relieved, too, that he wouldn't be at the party today. He'd planned to come, but his flight from Rio had been indefinitely delayed because of volcanic ash in the air. Fate was being kind to her for once.

Scarlet knew it was silly of her to feel awkward about seeing John Mitchell again. But she did.

To be fair, he was not an easy guy to be around at the best of times. Despite being a very good-looking man, John's social graces left a lot to be desired. Had a brilliant brain, though; this Scarlet knew first-hand, since they'd always been in the same classes at school, right from kindergarten through to their final exams. But being classmates and neighbours had not made them friends. John had never played with the other kids in the street, despite Scarlet asking him more than once. All he'd cared about was studying and surfing—the beach was a relatively short walk away.

Scarlet recalled how John had bitterly resented being asked by her mother to mind her on the school bus when bullying had become rife. Admittedly, he'd done it, even to the extent of fighting with another boy who had called her a foul name. He'd got suspended for a day over that, and a bloody nose as well, which hadn't exactly endeared her to him. Not that he had said anything directly to her. But when she'd thanked him, he'd scowled. Scowling at her was something he'd done quite often back then. She remembered once going to him for help with a maths problem in high school—he really had been terrific at maths—only to be told bluntly to stop being so bloody lazy and work it out for herself. Naturally, she hit back—Scarlet was not a girl to accept such rudeness meekly—screaming at him that she thought he was the meanest, most horrible boy she'd ever met and she would never ever ask him for help again, even if she were dying. A rather over-dramatic declaration, but she'd meant it at the time.

After graduating, John had gone on to Sydney university to become a geologist. She'd hardly ever seen him after that. He'd gone overseas to work once he had his degree, and only darkened his family's doorstep around Christmas, when he would stay for a week or two at most. Even then, he spent most of his time surfing by himself.

He did deign to attend the Christmas street-party which they held every year, and where their paths inevitably crossed. And, whilst John wasn't openly rude to her any more, their con-versations were hardly warm or communicative.

What she knew about his life was gleaned via his mother who belonged to the same quilting group as Scarlet's mother. According to Carolyn Mitchell, her son had become extremely wealthy in recent years after finding oil in Argentina and natural gas in some other South American country. He'd also bought a house in Rio, so it seemed likely that he wasn't coming home to Australia to live any time soon.

And wasn't getting married any time soon, either, Scarlet warranted. Loners like John didn't get married.

However, Scarlet had no doubt there was a woman—or women—in his life. Good-looking guys with money to burn didn't do without sex, even if they were antisocial bastards with about as much personal charm as a rattlesnake!

The bitchiness of this last thought startled Scarlet. It wasn't like her to be bitchy.

John Mitchell brought out the worst in her. But she really hated the way he didn't need anybody; hated his self-containment. She couldn't imagine John Mitchell ever having his heart broken. His heart was as hard as one of his precious rocks.

'Better get a move on, Scarlet,' her mother called through the bathroom door. 'It's twelve-twenty-five.'

After giving herself a vigorous mental shake,

Scarlet hurried back to her bedroom, where she quickly hooked a pair of silver and crystal drops through her earlobes, then bolted back to the living room where her mother was waiting for her, dressed in a tailored cream trouser suit with a caramel-coloured blouse underneath.

'You know, Mum,' she said, looking her mother up and down. 'You don't look a day over fifty.' Yet she'd turned sixty-two last birthday.

'Thank you, darling. And you don't look a day over twenty.'

'That's because I have great genes,' Scarlet replied.

'True,' Janet agreed, though the thought did occur to her that maybe her daughter had inherited one particular gene which wasn't as desirable as a youthful face, good skin and a slender figure—she herself had found it very difficult to get pregnant, which was why she'd only had the one child. It surprised her that a girl as intelligent as Scarlet hadn't asked her about that. But she hadn't, and Janet wasn't about to mention it. Not today.

'Come on, let's go,' Janet said instead, and picked up the present from the kitchen counter. Inside the rather exquisite red box was a ruby-coloured water jug and matching glasses which she'd found in a local antique shop and which she knew Carolyn would love. Martin probably wouldn't, but then Martin was one of those men who didn't enthuse over anything much. Except his grandson. There was no doubting that Melissa's little boy, Oliver, was the apple of his grandfather's eye. 'I won't need a jacket, will I?' Scarlet asked her.

'I shouldn't think so. Besides, it's not as though you have far to walk if you do get cold.'

'You're right. In that case, I won't take a handbag, either. Here, let me hold the present whilst you lock up.'

They went out the front way, Scarlet glad to see that the early cloud had lifted, letting the June sun do a decent job of warming up the air. Winter had not long arrived down under, but it had already been one of the coldest in a decade. And the wettest. Fortunately, the rain had stayed away today, which meant they wouldn't be confined indoors at the party. By the look of the number of cars already parked up and down the street, this was going to be a well-attended affair. There was nothing worse, in Scarlet's opinion, than having lots of people jammed into a couple of rooms. Admittedly, the Mitchells' two-storeyed home was very spacious, with large open-planned living areas. But even so…

'They've been lucky with the weather,' she remarked to her mother as they walked together across the road.

'Indeed. I...'

Whatever her mother was going to say was cut off by the Mitchells' house. The front door was reefed open and Carolyn ran out, looking flushed but happy.

'You'll never guess what's happened,' she said excitedly. 'I've just received a call from John. His plane was able to take off last night after all. Admittedly, a few hours late, but because of favourable winds they made good time and landed at Mascot a couple of hours ago. He tried to ring me earlier but I was on the phone so he hopped on a train. Anyway, he's going to be arriving at Gosford station in about twenty minutes. The train's just pulled into Woy Woy station. He said he'd catch a taxi, but you know how scarce they can be on a Sunday. So I told him to wait outside the station on the Mann Street side and I'd get someone to pick him up.

'Of course, he said that I shouldn't bother, but I said what tommyrot, that if he could fly here all the way from Brazil we could at least pick him up from the station. But once I hung up, I began thinking who I could ask. I couldn't very well leave my guests and I didn't like to ask Martin. Then I saw you two through the front window, and I thought who better than Scarlet? You don't mind, do you, dear?'

What could Scarlet possibly say?

Scarlet forced a smile and said, 'It would be my pleasure.'

CHAPTER TWO

THE train trip from Sydney to Gosford was a very pleasant one, once you left the city, especially if the train was half-empty and you were able to get an upstairs window seat on the right side, which John had. After crossing the Hawkesbury River, the track followed the water in long leisurely curves, giving even the weariest traveller a panoramic and relaxing ride.

Not that John was weary. That was the advantage of flying first class; you could sleep on board and arrive at your destination, refreshed and ready for anything.

Which was just as well, given what he would have to endure today.

Parties were not John's favourite pastime. He wasn't much of a drinker and didn't care for empty chit-chat. But it had been impossible not to come to his parents' fortieth wedding anniversary. He loved his mother dearly and would not hurt her for the world.

His father, however, was another matter entirely. It was difficult to love a parent who'd rejected you when you were only a child.

Nevertheless, John *did* still love his father, a discovery he'd made when his mother had rung him recently to tell him that his father had had a heart scare. John had actually been relieved that his old man hadn't died. He'd actually *cared*.

There was no getting over the fact, however, that what his father had done all those years ago had hurt him terribly. Thank God he'd had Grandpa. If it hadn't been for his grandfather stepping in, then Lord knew where he would have ended up. He'd probably have run away from home and been living on the streets. Maybe even ended up in jail. That was how wretched he'd felt after his brother had died. Wretched, confused and angry.

Yes, he'd become very angry. Sometimes, when he looked back over his teenage years, he felt guilty over the mean way he'd acted, especially how he'd been to Scarlet.

He'd been extra-mean to her.

But that was because he'd liked her so much. It had been perverse of him; he could see that now. But back then feeling anything for anyone scared the hell out of him. He didn't want to like her, or need her. So he'd pushed her away right from the first time she'd rocked up at his front door and asked him to come out and play. Not that she took no for an answer easily. Scarlet had always been a stubborn child with a will of iron. But she'd got the message in the end and had stopped asking him to come out and play. Perversely again, he'd been deeply hurt by her perfectly understandable rejection, deciding childishly that if she was going to ignore him, then he would ignore her.

Anything she could do he could do better!

Unfortunately, they had always been put into the same class—the 'gifted' class—so ignoring her totally had been a bit difficult. But he did his best. He hadn't been able to believe his bad luck when they'd been put in the same classes in high school. But worse had been yet to come. During that first year, puberty had struck both of them. Overnight, Scarlet had gone from a pretty but skinny little thing to a seriously hot-looking babe, whereas he had gone from an okay-looking boy into a too-thin, too-tall streak of hormone-muddled misery. Once the testosterone had started charging through his veins, however, he had begun fancying Scarlet like mad, which naturally had made him act even worse around her. But, privately, he had fantasised about being her boyfriend.

No no, let's not sugar-coat this, John. You didn't fantasise about that. You never wanted to be Scarlet's boyfriend. Being her boyfriend would have required a degree of emotional intimacy, something you were incapable of. Still are, if truth be told. You just wanted to have sex with her.

John smiled wryly to himself at the thought of how Scarlet would react if he ever confessed to lusting after her when they'd been at school together. Not that he ever intended telling her. What would be the point? She'd made it patently clear to him over the years that she couldn't stand him. Not that he blamed her. He'd started the hostility between them.

It was one of the many things he regretted now. She really was a lovely—if somewhat spoiled—girl, and hadn't deserved the way he treated her. Hadn't deserved getting conned by Jason Heath, either. Telling her the truth about that bastard was one thing he didn't regret. Scarlet might have ended up feeling miserable in the short term, but she'd have been even unhappier in the long term if he'd let her remain ignorant. He hadn't really loved Scarlet, he'd just been using her to hide behind.

John wondered if Scarlet would be at the party today. He wouldn't mind catching up with her and seeing how she was. His mother had told him during one of her phone calls that Scarlet had been inconsolable after finding out that Jason had been cheating on her—apparently, that was the story she'd put around to explain her broken engagement. Scarlet's teachers hadn't been the only ones to be shocked when she hadn't gone on to university. He'd been appalled, and had told her so on one occasion. After all, she was as smart as he was!

John chuckled wryly at himself, recognising his arrogance. At least he didn't strut around like some men, bragging about his successes. Bianca used to say that he was the strong, silent type.

John's heart contracted fiercely as it always did when he thought of Bianca. One day, perhaps, he would get over her death. But not yet. The memory was still too raw, too painful. One thing was sure, though—he would never go back to Brazil. That part of his life was over. For the next couple of years at least, he would live and work in Australia. Not here on the Central Coast, however. Aside from the fact it was hardly the mining capital of the world, he was never comfortable spending time at home. Too much bad karma.

No, he would base himself in Darwin, where he already owned an apartment and where he stayed for a few weeks each year. Not that his family knew about any of that. If he'd told them he holidayed here in Australia every winter, they would have been offended that he hadn't visited, or asked them to join him—his mother especially—so he'd simply never told them.

But he'd have to tell them something soon, he supposed. Though not the total truth, of course.

Over the past couple of weeks, John had tidied up all his loose ends in Rio. He'd given away his house to Bianca's family, as well as everything in it. He wanted no memories of his life there. All he'd taken with him to the airport was his wallet, his passport and his phones, plus the clothes on his back. During his long wait to board his flight—which had turned out to be even longer than he'd anticipated—he'd bought a small winter wardrobe at one of the many boutiques. He'd also used the opportunity to have his thick dark hair clippered again in the close-cropped style he'd become used to since being in hospital last year. One of the nurses had become frustrated with his increasingly shaggy mane and shaved it off to less than a centimetre all over his head. Despite having worn his hair longish all his life, John found he rather liked the buzz-cut look. It suited him and was easy to look after. He didn't even have to own a comb. John always liked to travel light.

The train pulling into Point Clare station brought his mind back to the present. In a few minutes they'd be at Gosford station. He wondered idly who would be picking him up. Not his father, that was for sure. Maybe Melissa. Or Leo, Melissa's husband. Yes, probably Leo.

He liked Leo. He was one of the good guys. Anyone who'd married his little sister had to be. Melissa was, without doubt, the most spoiled girl he'd ever known. Even more spoiled than Scarlet.

Scarlet again…

It would be good if she was at the party. Good to know if she'd finally forgiven him for telling her about Jason. But he rather doubted it. When news was bad, people liked to blame the messenger. Scarlet had been furious with him that night, calling him a liar at first. She'd finally calmed down enough to listen to what he was saying, but he suspected he was still not her favourite person. But then, he never had been, had he?

The announcement that they were approaching Gosford station had several people in the carriage standing up and making their way down to the doors at the lower level. John knew there was no need to hurry so he stayed where he was, gazing out at the expanse of almost-still water on his right, and the many boats moored there, bobbing gently up and down. Spread out around this expanse of water lay Gosford, the gateway to the Central Coast beaches, but not a beach town in itself, the sea being a few kilometres away. The train rumbled over a bridge then went past Blue-Tongue Stadium which had been a park in the old days but now hosted football matches and the occasional rock concert. Soon, they were pulling into the station where John took his time alighting.

It was a habit he'd got into when coming home, being slow to get off the train, doing everything he could to shorten the time of his visits. He still wasn't looking forward to today, but he no longer felt the gut-wrenching tension he used to feel at the prospect of being around his father. Which was a good thing. Not that he intended to stay too long. Masochism was not his style!

No one was there, waiting for him at the spot where his mother had instructed him to go, so he dropped his bag by his feet and waited. Less than thirty seconds later, a shiny blue Hyundai hatchback zoomed up the ramp and braked to a halt beside him.

He didn't recognise the car. But he recognised the beautiful blonde behind the wheel.

It was Scarlet.

CHAPTER THREE

You could have knocked Scarlet over with a feather once she realised that the gorgeous man standing at the five-minute pick-up spot, dressed in snug-fitting black jeans, black T-shirt and a black leather bomber jacket, was actually John Mitchell. It was a realisation that didn't come instantly, not even when he stepped forward and tapped on her passenger window. She'd thought he was some stranger wanting directions.

But as soon she wound down the window and he took off his wrap-around sunglasses, the penny dropped.

'My God, *John*!' she gasped as she stared into his familiar blue eyes.

'Yup,' he agreed. 'It's me.'

Scarlet could not believe how different he looked without long hair. Not better looking— he'd always been good-looking—but way more masculine. Without the softening effect of his hair, his facial features came into sharper focus:

his high cheekbones. His long strong nose. His square jawline. Of course the clothes he was wearing added to the macho image. Scarlet wasn't used to seeing John dressed in anything other than board shorts and T-shirts, his visits home long having been confined to summer. And, whilst she already knew he had a good body, there was something about a man dressed all in black that was very, very sexy.

Once she realised her staring was tipping into ogling, an embarrassed Scarlet swiftly pulled herself together.

'I didn't recognise you there for a moment,' she said brusquely. 'What happened to all your hair?'

He shrugged, then ran a slow hand over his near-smooth head, the action sending an erotically charged frisson running down Scarlet's spine.

'It was easier to look after,' he said. 'Where do you want me to put my bag? On the back seat, or right in the back?'

'Whatever,' she said, her offhand attitude a defensive reaction to her underlying shock at the situation. She wasn't used to finding John sexually attractive. It was highly irritating. There she'd been on the way in, thinking how awkward driving him home would be, only to find that it was going to be extra-awkward now. She hoped he hadn't noticed anything untoward. She would have to make sure she didn't act any differently with him from usual. No way was she going to compliment him on either his haircut, or his clothes, reminding herself forcibly that, underneath his sexy new facade, he was still the same selfish, rude, antisocial bastard who'd given her hell over the years.

'Mum shouldn't have asked you to do this,' he said as he climbed into the passenger seat and shut the door after him. 'I could easily have caught a taxi.' And he nodded towards the taxi rank ahead where several taxis stood, waiting for fares.

'No pointing in worrying about it now,' Scarlet said as she drove past them.

'I guess not,' he agreed. 'This is more pleasant than a taxi, anyway. Thank you, Scarlet.'

She could not have been more taken aback. Not only did John look different, he was acting different too. She almost asked what had happened to him in the eighteen months since he'd last graced home, but decided not to go down such a personal road. He might start asking her what had been happening to her. No way was she going to tell John Mitchell anything! Best keep any chit-chat in the car strictly superficial.

'Your parents have been lucky with the weather,' she said as she drove down the almost deserted main street of Gosford. 'This is the first decent day we've had so far this winter.'

He said nothing in return, for which she was grateful. But his silence didn't last for long.

'Mum tells me you haven't met anyone else,' he said when they stopped at a set of lights at East Gosford.

'No,' came her rather terse reply.

'I'm sorry, Scarlet. I know how much you've always wanted to get married and have a family.'

Her head whipped around, her face flushing with a sudden spurt of anger. 'Well, if you know that, then you shouldn't have said anything to me about Jason. If you hadn't, I would have been none the wiser, and I would have been married by now. Instead, I...'

Scarlet broke off when she felt tears sting her eyes, her knuckles showing white as she gripped the steering wheel tight and battled for composure.

John was appalled at the level of Scarlet's distress. Appalled and sympathetic, but not guilty.

'I am truly sorry, Scarlet,' he repeated. 'But I had no choice in the matter. I couldn't let you marry a man who was just using you.'

'There are worse things to happen to a woman than having a gay husband,' she threw at him.

'He didn't love you, Scarlet.'

'How on earth could you know a thing like that?'

'Because he told me.'

'You!'

'Yes. I felt sorry for him—he was too scared to publicly accept who he was. Even I wasn't as lonely or lost as that.'

Scarlet was moved by the grim bleakness in John's voice and the stark reality of what he'd just revealed.

'The lights are green, Scarlet.'

'What? Oh yes, so they are.'

She drove on, her thoughts muddled by the sudden sympathy she felt for the man sitting next to her. Who would have believed it? First, she'd started finding John incredibly sexy. Now she was feeling sorry for him as well. Life could be very perverse, she decided.

'So why *haven't* you found anyone else?' John persisted.

Scarlet sighed a sigh of sheer frustration. The one thing she could have depended on with John in the past was his brooding silences. Now, suddenly, he was turning into a conversationalist! And there she'd been, thinking she wouldn't have to answer any awkward questions today.

'I've stopped looking, okay?' she replied somewhat aggressively. 'I could ask you the same question, you know,' she swept on, always having been skilled at the art of verbal counter-attack. She hadn't been captain of the debating team at school for nothing! 'Why is it that *you've* never found anyone? No one you dared to bring home, that is.'

He laughed. John Mitchell actually laughed. Things were getting seriously weird here.

'Come now, Scarlet, you know my mother. If I brought a girl home, she would immediately start wanting to know when the wedding was.'

'I could tell her that. It would be never!'

'You know me too well, Scarlet.'

'I know you well enough to know you're not interested in marriage. If you were, you'd be married by now. You'd have no trouble finding a wife.'

'Thank you for the compliment,' he said. 'But you're right. Marriage is not for me.'

'That's still no reason not to bring a girl home occasionally.'

'I can't agree with you on that score. There's enough tension whenever I come home as it is.'

This was true, Scarlet conceded. John and his father didn't get along. She'd always blamed John for this; he'd been such a difficult boy. But she now wondered if there'd been some secret reason for John's antisocial attitude, something which might have happened before they'd come to live in her street. He certainly wasn't being his usual gruff self with her right at this moment. Frankly, he'd spoken more words to her since getting into her car five minutes ago than he had over their whole lifetime together! Curiosity demanded she use this uncharacteristic chattiness to find out some more about his personal life.

'Do you have anyone back in Brazil at the moment?' she asked, glancing his way.

His face, which had been open and smiling, suddenly closed up again.

'I did have,' he answered. 'Till recently.'

'I'm sorry,' she said quite sincerely, and wondered what had happened.

'So am I,' he said. 'Now, that's enough personal information for one day.'

Scarlet's teeth clenched hard in her jaw. She should have known that his being nice and normal wouldn't last.

'Why didn't you keep going straight along the main road?' he asked when she swung right onto Terrigal Drive. 'It's quicker.'

'Not any more, it isn't. It's suffering from terminal roadworks. If you came home a little more often, you would know that,' she pointed out somewhat waspishly. 'Apart from that, I'm the driver here. You're the passenger. The passenger does not tell the driver where and how to drive. That's bad manners.'

He laughed again, though this time it had a

harsher sound. 'Glad to see you haven't changed, Scarlet.'

'I was just thinking the same about you. You might look different, John Mitchell—you're certainly dressing a damned sight better—but deep down, you're still the same obnoxious boy who thinks he's smarter than everyone else.'

This time he made no come-back, leaving Scarlet to feel totally ashamed of herself. She'd overreacted, as usual. She'd always had a quick temper, especially around John.

'I'm sorry,' she said swiftly into the uncomfortable silence. 'That was very rude of me.'

'Oh, I don't know,' he said, surprising her with a wry little smile. 'It wasn't far off the truth. I can be quite arrogant.'

She couldn't help it. She smiled back at him.

Their eyes met for a long moment, Scarlet being the first to look away, John's eyes still on her as she struggled to put her mind back on her driving. It kept rattling her, this sudden attraction between them.

'Will you stop staring at me?' she snapped at last, but without looking his way.

'I wasn't staring,' he denied. 'I was just looking and thinking.'

'About what?'

'Don't forget there's a speed camera just along here.'

Scarlet rolled her eyes. 'For pity's sake, John, I *live* here twenty-four-seven. I know about the speed camera.'

'Then why are you doing nearly fifty?'

'I can do fifty. It's not a school day.'

'The sign said forty. Roadworks ahead.'

Scarlet jammed on her brakes. Just in time, too.

'If they dig up one more road around here,' she muttered, 'I'm going to scream.'

'No screaming,' John said in droll tones. 'Can't abide screaming women.'

When she glared over at him, Scarlet was astounded to find him smiling at her.

'John Mitchell,' she said, her mouth twitching. 'You've actually found a sense of humour.'

'I have today, it seems. Which is just as well. I'm almost home.'

Which they were.

The street where Scarlet lived was no different from most streets on the Central Coast, full of a motley collection of houses of all different shapes and sizes. It was a family-friendly street where the inhabitants actually stayed put, rather than moving every seven years or so, as seemed to be ingrained in the Australian psyche. Of course, it *was* in Terrigal, which had been voted recently one of the ten most desirable places in the world to live.

It would be difficult to find anywhere better to bring up a family. Admittedly, they didn't have ocean or lagoon views in their street, but that made the houses more reasonably priced. They still enjoyed the wonderfully mild climate which came from living near the sea. On top of that they were so close to everything, not just the beach. Erina Fair shopping centre was only a ten minute drive away and Sydney a little over an hour.

Scarlet could never understand why John didn't come home more often.

'Looks like a big turn-out,' John said once Scarlet turned the corner into their street.

'You have your mother to blame for that. If she didn't put on such a good spread, she wouldn't get so many people accepting her invitations. It's always like this when it's your family's turn for the Christmas party. Look, there's your mum and sister on the front porch, waiting for you.' No father, though, she noted. 'I'll just stop in our driveway and you can get out. I want to put the car in the garage.'

'Fine,' he agreed, hopping out and taking his bag from the back seat before slapping the car on the roof and shouting thanks to her.

She pressed the remote for the garage door, watching John in the rear-vision mirror whilst she waited for the door to roll its way slowly upwards. He really did look amazing today. Great buns in those jeans. Great body all round. If he'd been anybody else, she might have been tempted to flirt with him.

Just the thought made her laugh. *Flirt* with John Mitchell? What would be the point in that?

Scarlet laughed again. She was still amused over the idea when she returned to the party.

CHAPTER FOUR

SCARLET looked for John straight away. When she couldn't spot him anywhere amongst the crowd of partygoers who'd all gathered under the outdoor entertaining area, she wandered back inside the house. But the only person she found there was his mother, getting a couple of bottles of wine out of the fridge. The large open-plan living room was empty of people, with no sign of John anywhere.

'Ah, Scarlet,' his mother said. 'Thank you so much for getting John. It was very good of you.'

'No trouble, Mrs Mitchell. Where is he, by the way?'

'Upstairs in his bedroom,' Carolyn retorted, sounding a bit annoyed. 'Said he had to go get my anniversary present but I think he's just avoiding talking to people. Look, could I bother you to go up there and bring him down? All the food is ready. You look lovely today, by the way, dear,' Carolyn rattled on before Scarlet could accept or reject the request.

Strangely, she didn't mind the mission. It would give her the chance to see if he still had all those girlie posters over his walls.

He didn't. The room was stripped bare of all boyish paraphernalia. John was standing by the window, staring down at the street, his bedroom being at the front of the house. His bag had been slung on top of the bed, unopened. Scarlet glanced around but couldn't see any present anywhere.

'I've been sent to bring you downstairs,' she called from the open doorway.

He turned from the window and smiled a rueful smile. 'Poor Scarlet,' came his ironic remark. 'You've been given all the awful jobs today.'

She didn't deny it. The strange truth, however, was that she hadn't minded driving him home as much as she'd thought she would. And she didn't really mind coming up here to collect him. But she wasn't about to tell him that.

'Did you find your mother's present?'

'I did,' he said, and patted the right hip pocket of his leather jacket.

'Something small and sinfully expensive?'

'Could be.'

'Let me guess—a real ruby.' What else would

a geologist son give to his mother on her ruby wedding anniversary?

'You always were a clever little minx.'

'And you always were a sarcastic bastard.'

He scowled at her for a second, then smiled. 'I tell you what. I promise to go down and face the small talk if you promise not to leave my side.'

'And what, pray tell, do *I* get out of that deal?'

His smile broadened. 'My suddenly sparkling company?'

'Not good enough, I'm afraid. I have no faith in your company becoming suddenly sparkling. I will need more of a bribe than that.'

'Would a real diamond do the trick?'

Scarlet wasn't sure if he was serious, or just teasing her. Whatever, she was tempted to do some teasing of her own.

'I have no use for a diamond,' she replied haughtily. 'Unless it's sitting atop a band of gold and comes with a proposal of marriage.'

The look on his face was priceless.

'No?' she went on saucily. 'Pity. You're not bad looking, after all. And you're filthy rich. Not to mention not gay. What more could a girl possibly want?'

'Nice try, Scarlet. You had me going there for a while.'

She grinned. 'I did, didn't I? Revenge *is* sweet.'

'Revenge for what?'

'For all the times you made me want to kill you.'

'Mea culpa,' he said, his tone droll.

'You're right there. But today is meant to be a happy day, so I'll put aside my petty grievances and do what you ask, without payment of any kind. Not that I thought you meant to give me a diamond for real.'

'If I did, you've missed out now. Still, be a nice, sweet, agreeable companion for the rest of the day and I might give you one.'

'In your dreams, lover.'

He laughed. 'You're right there, Scarlet.'

John knew full well that that was one thing he would never be—Scarlet's lover. Which was a pity. She looked utterly gorgeous today in that purple and black outfit. Shame she wasn't one of those girls who could enjoy a fling without always looking for a ring on their finger in return.

But that was the way she was and nothing would ever change that. Which was also a pity. John suspected one of the reasons Scarlet hadn't found her Mr Right was because she had 'desperately seeking marriage' written all over her. What she needed to do, in his opinion, was lighten up.

Perhaps he would tell her that later today if he found the right opportunity.

'Come on,' he said, flashing Scarlet a warm

smile as he hooked her arm through his. 'Time to get ourselves downstairs before they send out a search party.'

CHAPTER FIVE

SCARLET could not believe how much she enjoyed the party, and John's company, though she would not go so far as to say he'd 'sparkled'. After giving his delighted mother her ruby—which was uncut but simply enormous—he'd actually deigned to make a small speech, praising his parents' fortitude in staying married for so long and wishing them all the best for the future. Then, even more surprising, after the buffet luncheon was over he'd made the effort to talk to his father. It had been a slightly awkward conversation—Scarlet had been hovering nearby at the time—but it was Martin Mitchell who'd sounded the more awkward, she thought, after which the fool had spent the rest of the afternoon playing with Melissa's little boy. Admittedly, Oliver was a delightful child, with a highly engaging personality. But still, one would have thought Martin could have afforded to spend some more time with a son who'd flown all the way from South America to be with his parents on their special day.

Scarlet had felt seriously annoyed with the man, which made her even more solicitous towards John. She also downed a good few glasses of wine, which she had a tendency to do when she was upset. Being tipsy brought out the flirtatious side in her, which was helped by the fact that he invariably sought her out if she left his side for too long, whispering to her each time that she wouldn't get a diamond if she kept deserting her post.

By five-thirty, the party was winding down, with people gradually leaving. By six, the Mitchell place was almost empty of guests, and Scarlet and her mother stayed back to help Carolyn and Melissa clean up. Oliver had been put down for a nap, whilst the men—Martin, John and Leo—had retired to the living room to watch the evening news on TV.

'I had my four-month ultrasound on Friday,' Melissa said out of the blue as she and Scarlet were restacking the dishwasher together. Their mothers were outside at the time, piling up more dirty plates to carry in.

Scarlet stiffened as she always did these days when girls she knew started talking about their pregnancies. She'd known Melissa was pregnant again, but the subject hadn't come up that day as yet.

'Oh?' she managed to reply as casually as she could manage. 'Everything well, I hope?'

'Marvellous. Leo was there with me, of course. He actually cried when they told him it was a little girl. So did I. Oliver's a darling boy, but there's something about little girls, isn't there?'

Scarlet was on the verge of tears herself. She didn't give a damn if she had a girl or a boy. She just wanted a baby.

'Would you like to see the pictures of the ultrasound?' Melissa asked her. 'I brought them with me to show Mum. They're just upstairs. I'll go get them,' she added before Scarlet could say yes or no.

John saw the stricken look on Scarlet's face the moment he walked into the kitchen.

'What is it?' he asked straight away. 'What's happened?'

'I have to get out of here,' she muttered.

Too late. Melissa was back in a flash with the dreaded pictures. Scarlet had no choice but to look at them and make all the right noises, for how could she do anything else without making a complete fool of herself? Melissa insisted John look at them too, which he did, though he didn't gush, for which Scarlet was grateful. At some stage, their respective mothers re-entered the kitchen. Scarlet now had to endure Carolyn Mitchell raving on about how lucky Melissa was to be having a little girl and how lucky they were as grandparents to have their daughter living so close. She then added that it was obvious they were never going to get any grandchildren from John and, even if by some miracle they did, they'd probably never see them, since he preferred to live in South America than Australia.

John had no idea what had distressed Scarlet earlier, but he suspected—by the look on her face—that she still wanted out. He did, too. Hell, yes. And the sooner the better.

'Sorry to love you and leave you, folks,' he said once his mother stopped to draw breath. 'But I asked Scarlet out tonight and she said yes. So if you don't mind, we'll be off.' So, saying, he took hold of a startled Scarlet and steered her firmly towards the front door. 'Don't wait up,' he called over his shoulder, then whispered in her ear. 'We'll have to take your car, as I don't have one here, but don't worry; I can drive. I've only had two light beers all afternoon.'

Scarlet would have agreed to anything he said at that moment, she was so grateful to be away from Melissa and the pictures of her baby.

Five minutes later, John was reversing her car out of their garage, Scarlet only then realising she'd have a lot of questions to answer when she finally got home that night.

'Nice wheels, Scarlet,' John said once they were underway. 'The last time I was home you were driving an old white rust bucket.'

'I decided to spoil myself this year,' she replied. New car and a baby. At least that *had* been the plan.

Suddenly, the tears which had been threatening ever since Melissa brought up the subject of her pregnancy came back with a vengeance. Scarlet tried to choke them back but it was way too late. Maybe if she'd cried earlier in the week when she'd realised she hadn't conceived, she might have stood a chance of controlling her emotion. Instead, it had been building up in her for days, this feeling of helplessness and hopelessness. She'd tried so hard to stay positive. So very hard.

Her head dropped into her hands as her shoulders started to shake, noisy sobs bursting from her lungs.

John didn't know what to do for a split second. He'd known Scarlet was upset over something but he hadn't expected this level of grief. It wasn't like Scarlet at all!

To keep on driving seemed heartless so he pulled over to the side of the road and switched off the engine.

He didn't try to comfort her physically. It was too darned awkward in a small car with the gear stick and hand brake between the front seats. So he just sat there and let her weep. Bianca had once told him that women needed a good cry occasionally. Most times, they didn't require the men in their lives to solve their problems, just to be supportive and to listen. John wished he had a handkerchief to give her. But he wasn't the handkerchief-carrying kind of man.

Finally, when the weeping subsided, Scarlet snapped open the glove box and extracted a small box of tissues. She blew her dripping nose at length, then threw him a pained look.

'Thank you,' she sniffed.

'For what?'

'For getting me out of there.'

'Am I allowed to ask what upset you so much?'

'No,' she grumped, crumpling up the tissues into her hand and turning her face away from him.

'No?' John was never at his best when his will was thwarted. 'Scarlet King, we are not moving from this spot till you tell me what's going on.' As he made his stand, John's mind started running over what had happened after he'd walked into the kitchen. Melissa had come downstairs with the photographs of her ultrasound, insisting that they both look at them. Then his mother

walked in and made some crack about his never giving her grandchildren. Which was probably true.

But, John realised in what could only be described as a light-bulb moment, Scarlet wanted to give *her* mother grandchildren.

'It was because of Melissa's pregnancy,' he said with typical male satisfaction at having worked something out for himself.

The lack of sensitivity in John's tone—not to mention the underlying arrogance—brought Scarlet back to herself. Her head whipped round, her blue eyes glaring daggers at him.

'Yes, of course it was your precious sister's pregnancy which upset me,' she snapped. 'Plus the way she shoved those damned photographs in my face. How do you think I felt when she told me she was going to have a lovely little girl to go with her lovely little boy when I would give my right arm to have just one baby of any sex?'

'But you will, Scarlet. One day,' he added.

'Oh really? You can guarantee that, can you, John? I'm thirty-four years old. My biological clock is ticking away like a time bomb. Already the odds of my conceiving a child are going downhill. If I don't have a baby soon, I might never have one.'

'Don't be ridiculous, Scarlet. Women of forty and older are having babies all the time.'

'I'm not being ridiculous, and women over forty are *not* having babies all the time. Most of the older mothers you read about these days are celebrities and actresses who have access to the best fertility clinics in the world. Have you noticed how many of them are having twins? You don't honestly think they're being conceived naturally, do you?'

John hadn't really thought about it at all. 'I will bow to your better knowledge on the subject. But you're not over forty yet, Scarlet. Not by a long shot. There's no reason to panic.'

'I have *every* reason to panic.'

'Look, if you're so damned desperate to have children, then why don't you just go out and get yourself pregnant? You're gorgeous—you'll have all the offers you could want.'

Scarlet gave him a totally scandalised look, determinedly ignoring the fact that he thought she was gorgeous. 'You think I would risk falling pregnant to just anyone, potentially also risking my sexual health? No, thank you very much. I have no intention of doing that.'

'So you're just going to wait till Mr Right comes along?'

'Actually, John, I have no intention of doing that either.'

'Oh? And what, pray tell, *are* you going to do?'

'If you must know, I'm already doing it.'

'Already doing what?'

Scarlet knew she'd just backed herself into a corner. Her and her big mouth! John always did have this bad habit of making her want to bring him down in flames, which was very immature of her. They weren't bickering children or rival classmates any more. They were grown up people.

Suddenly, it didn't seem such a bad idea to tell him what she was up to. John wouldn't tell anyone else, not if she asked him not to. Frankly, it would be good to talk to someone other than her mother, someone more objective. John was an intelligent guy; he would see the sense in her plan. Scarlet needed reassurance at that moment that she was doing the right thing.

'The thing is, John,' she said, still slightly hesitant. 'I… Um… I've decided to have a baby by artificial insemination.'

When he said nothing, she turned her face to look at him. He was frowning, like he didn't understand the concept at all.

'I investigated it thoroughly on the Internet first,' she rattled on, feeling compelled to explain it more fully. 'Trust me when I say I've given this a lot of thought and research. Anyway, I found a local clinic where they had a whole catalogue of sperm donors to choose from. All their background information was listed: their physical characteristics, health records, intelligence levels. I picked one out which I liked the sound of. He's American, tall, good-looking, with dark hair, blue eyes and an IQ of a hundred and thirty. Some of them had higher IQs—most of the donors are university students—but I didn't want a child who was a genius, just one smart enough to do well in life without having to struggle.'

'If you've already decided on this course of action, Scarlet,' John said when she finally stopped talking, 'then why were you so upset over Melissa's pregnancy?'

Scarlet sighed. 'I guess you might as well know the rest. The thing is it hasn't worked so far. I've failed to fall pregnant twice now and I... I... Well, when Melissa showed me her ultrasound pictures, I began to worry that something was wrong with me and I would never be a mother, and I... I...' Scarlet broke off when she choked up again.

'For what it's worth, Scarlet,' John said quietly into the sudden silence, 'I admire that you've taken positive action to get what you want in life. You have courage. At the same time,' John couldn't help himself from telling her, 'I think you're being quite selfish in deliberately having a child who will be denied a father figure in his life.'

Scarlet was both astonished and angered by

this unexpected criticism. 'I wouldn't say that having a father figure in life is the be-all and end-all. I would have thought that you, of all people, would appreciate that.'

'*Touché*. But I did have a grandfather. Your baby won't even have that.'

'Maybe not, but it will have a wonderful grandmother.' Only one, though, she realised. Her paternal grandparents had both died some years ago.

'True,' John agreed. 'But what about when she's gone? What then?'

'I can't think about then,' Scarlet snapped.

'Just like your fictional name-sake.'

She glared at him. 'I thought you would understand.'

John shrugged. He wasn't sure why he found the idea of Scarlet having a baby with Mr IQ-of-a-hundred-and-thirty so uncomfortable, but his whole body objected.

'Wanting a baby is not exactly complicated. It's a basic drive in most women. And quite a lot of men too, I'm told,' she added caustically.

'I dare say you're right. Look, it's obvious that you're determined on this course of action, so I have a suggestion to make which I think would be infinitely preferable to your being impregnated by some stranger who will impart nothing to your child's life but a set of genes, which may not be as desirable as they read on paper. After all, what do you really know about this sperm donor? Nothing of any depth, that's for sure. You don't know his background or his family or his mental health. Perhaps it is a blessing that you haven't conceived his child so far.'

Scarlet could not believe that John was being so negative. All life had some risk, didn't it? There was no such a thing as a perfect plan, or a perfect partner, or a perfect anything! She had no idea what his counter-suggestion was going to be, but if he thought she was going to change her mind about trying for a baby then he was delusional.

John knew that what he was about to propose would shock her. He was pretty shocked at it himself. But something deep inside him was driving him on—the thought of Scarlet having a baby to some anonymous stranger was repulsive. She deserved better than that. She deserved...

'So, Scarlet, in the interest of the future happiness and security of your offspring, I propose that you ditch your present sperm donor in favour of...me.'

Scarlet could not have been more shocked if he'd suggested immaculate conception. She just stared at him with rounded eyes, looking for the catch. Or the joke.

'You *have* to be kidding me!' she exclaimed at last.

'Actually, no,' he said, feel perversely pleased with his offer now that he'd made it. 'I'm not.'

'But... But... *Why*?'

'Why not? I qualify, don't I? I'm tall, reasonably good-looking, with dark hair and blue eyes. Unfortunately my IQ is a good bit over a hundred and thirty but that's a moot point. I promise I won't interfere with the way you bring up the child, so it won't be so different to what you had planned. Though I would like to see the child occasionally. On top of that, he or she'll have a second pair of grandparents living just across the road. And, whilst my father wasn't a great father, I saw today that he has the makings of a great grandfather. That can happen sometimes, you know. His father—my grandfather—admitted to being a pathetic parent but he came into his own as a grandparent.'

Scarlet shook her head from side to side. 'I'm having serious trouble taking this all in.'

'Take your time.'

Scarlet blinked, then frowned. 'I still can't see why you would offer to do this.'

'I am capable of kindness, you know.' Or so Bianca had believed.

'This is more than just being kind,' Scarlet said, trying to get her head around John's offer.

Who would have believed he would do such a thing? She shook her head from side to side. 'I have to confess that I'm tempted. Mum would certainly be more comfortable with you being the father than some stranger.'

'I would imagine so. She quite likes me, you know. Has done ever since I promised to look after you on the school bus.'

Scarlet rolled her eyes at him. 'I seem to recall you weren't thrilled at the time.'

'I didn't mind.'

'Rubbish! Come now, John, you've never been the Good Samaritan type. Which makes your offering to be my sperm donor all the more puzzling. Heavens, I don't know what to think or what to say.'

'Just say yes, Scarlet.'

'But it's such a difficult decision. I mean…it's a big thing to have a child together. Different if we were in love.'

John snorted. 'As we both know, being in love is no guarantee of future happiness. People fall out of love all the time.'

'It's still important for parents to like and respect each other.'

'You think I don't like and respect you?'

'We haven't exactly been the best of friends over the years.'

'But that's all in the past, when we were just stupid kids. We got along very well today, didn't we?'

'Yes,' she agreed reluctantly. 'Yes, we did. Oh Lord, I still don't know. If we go ahead and do this, what on earth are we going to tell everyone?'

'We'll cross that bridge when we come to it. Your priority at this point is becoming pregnant. Your body obviously isn't clicking with the sperm donor you chose,' he went on with cool, corrupting logic. 'You need to try someone different.'

Scarlet knew that, if she failed to get pregnant again with her chosen sperm donor, she'd regret not accepting John's offer. It was a case of do now, or possibly die childless!

'Okay. Okay. I'm going to throw caution to the winds and just say yes.'

'Great,' John said, feeling more excited than when he'd found oil. 'So what's the plan?'

'I'll contact the clinic first thing tomorrow morning and arrange for a time for you to go in and give them a sperm sample. Then, when—'

'Hang on!' John interrupted immediately. 'That's not how it's going to be done at all!'

'What do you mean?'

'I mean I have no intention of becoming a father via a turkey baster. Or a syringe. Or whatever they use these days. If we're doing this, let's do it right.'

'You mean you...you want to have sex with me?'

CHAPTER SIX

JOHN smiled wryly. 'Don't sound so shocked, Scarlet. I've wanted you since the first moment I saw you today, not to mention for years while we were growing up.'

Scarlet blushed furiously, shocked, yet secretly elated to discover that the feelings which had so blindsided her today had been returned for so long.

'But don't start thinking that I'm doing this just because of that—because I'm not.' Even as the denial left his mouth, John suspected he was morally skating on thin ice here. If what he was saying was strictly true, then why not just do what she suggested—go to this clinic and give them a sperm sample?

The truth was he *did* want to have sex with her. At the same time, he *did* also believe that normal intercourse was the best chance Scarlet had for falling pregnant. Clearly, the coldly clinical method hadn't worked. She needed to relax, to enjoy herself.

John decided to be bluntly honest with her. 'Not that I won't enjoy having sex with you,' he admitted. 'But that's not the only reason I'm suggesting we actually sleep with each other. It's because I think you're more likely to fall pregnant that way. Which is what you want, isn't it? To have a baby?'

John's saying the word 'baby' dragged Scarlet back to the present. She'd been off in another world ever since he'd confessed to wanting to have sex with her since they were teenagers. 'What? Oh yes, yes, that's what I want,' she said. 'A baby.'

'So what do you say, Scarlet?'

'I don't know...' The idea of actually sleeping with John made her head spin.

He sighed. 'What don't you know?'

'I don't know what I don't know!' she blurted out, feeling totally confused and conflicted.

'Look, I can understand that my suggestion has come as a bit of a shock to you, so why don't we go somewhere for coffee and talk about it rationally?'

'I don't think I'm capable of being rational about this. You've totally blown me away. I have to think about this on my own.'

John nodded. He wanted her to say yes with

a depth of desire which shocked him; something in him was demanding that he—and only he—should give Scarlet the baby she so desperately wanted. However, much as he hated it, she needed time.

'I'll take you home.'

Scarlet sighed. The idea of going home and facing her mother while she was trying to decide something so huge didn't appeal either.

'How about we drive to Erina Fair and see a movie? You can pick something you'll like, some macho action flick with lots of car chases and killings. You can get all involved in that whilst I sit in the dark and think.'

He laughed. 'You are such a sexist, Scarlet. I happen to like a wide range of movies, not just macho action flicks, as you put it.'

'Oh sure,' she said in droll tones.

'I'll prove it to you.'

He surprised her by choosing a romantic comedy, one of those friends-into-lovers plots which had become popular lately. Scarlet might have enjoyed it if there hadn't been so many sex scenes, all of which were extremely raunchy. Clothes were stripped off at regular intervals as the two friends had wildly uninhibited sex in every conceivable place and position: on the floor. On the sofa. In a lift. Even in a meadow.

Of course, each of them had perfectly toned

and buffed bodies which photographed beautifully from every angle; no doubt they were faking their orgasms. But still…it was obvious they knew what seriously fantastic ones felt like, and sounded like. Did people *really* make loud noises like that? Scarlet never had. Before long she began worrying that, if she agreed to John's proposal, he might expect her to be like that girl on the screen. And she wasn't, not even remotely. Her breasts were a lot smaller, for starters; her body wasn't as gym-bunny perfect and she certainly didn't come every single time. Actually, she didn't come very often at all, and never during actual sex. The ending annoyed her as well: it was pure Hollywood fiction where the protagonists fell in love and lived happily ever after. As if that ever happened!

'Is that what you're afraid of?' John said as they left the theatre. 'That if we have sex you might fall in love with me?'

Laughter spluttered from Scarlet's lips before she could smother it.

'Right,' he said drily. 'Obviously, that's not what you're afraid of.'

'No,' she said. Her fears had nothing to do with love. She stopped walking to turn and look up at him with thoughtful eyes. 'You have to admit that I don't really know the adult you, John. You're somewhat of a mystery man these days.'

'Not as much of a mystery man as your university student.'

'True. But I would still want to know more about your life in South America before I agreed to your being the father of my child. After all, your proposal is not the same kind of a deal as I would have had with my student donor. He doesn't want to be a part of my child's life. But you do, even if it is only in a limited way.'

'Okay, let's find a place to have some coffee and I'll tell you all about myself.' Even as he said this, John knew damned well he was not going to tell her the absolute truth. She could know about his work; nothing but good news there. Scarlet certainly didn't need to worry that he couldn't support a child financially. But no way was he going to tell her about Bianca. He could hardly bear to think about what had happened to that poor woman. Talking about it was out of the question.

Still, Scarlet would probably want some idea of his past love life. So he'd confess to a succession of girlfriends over the years, none of whom he'd fallen in love with, most of whom had broken up with him because of his inability to commit. That should do the trick of explaining his present partnerless existence, and did have a great deal of truth in it—though one could hardly call the sexual partners he'd had in the last decade 'girlfriends'.

'That pizza place over there looks open,' he said and took her arm.

Scarlet stiffened inside at his touch. Her whole body flared to life at the thought of how much more of her he would be touching if she agreed to his proposal. Just the thought of getting naked with him made butterflies erupt in her stomach.

Suddenly, she couldn't do it.

'No, John,' she said, and pulled her arm away from him.

'No what?'

'No, I've decided not to accept your offer. Thank you for making it; it was amazingly generous of you. But it's just not going to work for me. Please don't argue with me about this or tell me I'm being irrational. Because if you do I know I'm going to burst into tears again.' Which was true. Her emotions, already fragile, were in danger of embarrassing her once more.

She couldn't tell what John was thinking. His face had always been hard to read.

'I see,' was all he said. 'Well, it's your life, Scarlet. You do what you think best.'

'Thank you,' she said, struggling to keep the tears in check.

'No point in going for coffee then, is there?' he said brusquely. 'I'll take you home.'

CHAPTER SEVEN

SCARLET'S mother was still up watching television when she let herself into the house. Which perhaps was just as well. It stopped her breaking down, which was what stupidly she wanted to do again.

Her mother looked up at her from the sofa. 'You're home earlier than I expected.'

Scarlet glanced at the clock on the wall. It was only just after nine.

'Yes, well, there's not all that much to do around here on a Sunday night,' she said as she walked behind the kitchen counter and reached for the kettle. 'We didn't feel like eating or drinking any more so we went to a movie.'

'Any good?'

'So so,' she said, filling the kettle with water then turning it on. 'What movie are *you* watching?' Her mother always watched a movie at eight-thirty on a Sunday night.

'A very boring slice-of-life story which I'm

just about to turn off.' Which she did. 'If you're making tea, make one for me too, please.'

'Okay,' Scarlet said, thinking she really had to get herself to bed before the third degree began in earnest.

Janet twisted round on the sofa so that she could watch her daughter's face. 'I was surprised to see you getting on so well with John today.'

'So was I,' Scarlet agreed, quite truthfully.

'He hardly left your side all afternoon.' *And hardly took his eyes off you as well.* Though that wasn't entirely new. Janet had always thought John had a secret crush on Scarlet when they were at school. He just hadn't had the confidence back then to do anything about it. The man who'd asked Scarlet out tonight had been a different kettle of fish entirely. Janet had been taken aback at how good he'd looked when he'd arrived. Not all men suited having their hair cut so short but John did. He had a well-shaped head, flat ears and a handsome face. A nice body, too. All in all, a fine looking man. Unattached too, according to Carolyn.

'You don't think that…?'

'No, Mum,' Scarlet cut in forcefully. 'That's never going to happen between John and me, so please don't go there.'

Janet was not about to give up *that* easily. 'If

you say so, dear. But what does John say? Did he want to see you some more whilst he was home?'

'Mum, he only asked me out tonight because he can't stand being around his father for too long. I dare say he'll be flying back to where he came from immediately. My guess would be tomorrow.'

'Surely he'll stay a little longer than that after coming all the way from Brazil?'

Scarlet shrugged. 'I doubt it. Here's your tea, Mum. I'm taking mine to my room. I'm tired.'

Janet frowned as Scarlet went upstairs after coming out of the kitchen a few minutes later. She knew her daughter better than anyone else in this world. She could sense her state of mind, especially when she tried to hide it. Which she was doing right now.

Something had happened between her and John tonight, something which she didn't want to talk about, something which had made her very tense. Had he made a pass? Janet wondered. She wouldn't have been surprised if he had. Scarlet was lovely looking, but she had impossibly high standards when it came to men. They only had to put a single foot wrong and they were out the door. If Scarlet hadn't been searching for perfection in a partner, she would long have been married by now. Of course, Janet didn't condone men who were unfaithful the way Jason had been. But a girl sometimes had to turn a blind eye to minor failings if she wanted to become a wife and mother as much as Scarlet did.

Not that it mattered now, Janet thought with a resigned sigh. She'd obviously given up on the idea of marriage. Even if John *were* interested, he'd be fighting a losing battle with Scarlet. All she wanted was a baby.

Janet stood up from the sofa and walked over to pick up her tea. She hoped and prayed Scarlet would fall pregnant next month.

The same thought kept Scarlet awake long after she climbed into bed. She tossed and turned, her mind torturing herself with that most horrible 'what if?' What if she *didn't* fall pregnant next month? What then? Would she keep on trying or resort to more complicated and expensive procedures like IVF? How long could she keep doing this before she went stark, raving mad?

Already she could feel herself unravelling.

Maybe she should have accepted John's offer. Why *hadn't* she? Was it just because the idea of having sex with him terrified her? Was she so frightened of not living up to his expectations? That seemed a truly pathetic reason to knock back what was in many ways an excellent proposal. Then why, Scarlet? What are you so afraid of where John is concerned?

Her whirling mind eventually went back to that movie they'd seen tonight, with its truly cheesy ending. Surely she couldn't be afraid of something similar happening to her? It seemed ludicrous in the extreme to think she would fall for John just because she went to bed with him.

For the umpteenth time, Scarlet sat up and punched her pillow before turning it over and slumping back down again.

'I'm getting sick of this,' she muttered as she stared blankly up at the darkened ceiling. 'I have to go to work in the morning. It's all your fault, John Mitchell. You should have minded your own business. You don't really want to be the father of my baby. You don't really want to be the father of *any* baby. So why on earth did you make such a ridiculous offer in the first place? It just doesn't make sense!'

The man himself was thinking along those same lines as he stood at his bedroom window, staring down at Scarlet's house as he'd done so many times when he'd been a boy, wanting to join in as she played with the other kids.

A wry smile pulled at his face. Here he was, years later, still wanting Scarlet, though admittedly in quite a different way!

Okay, so his offering to be her sperm donor had begun as a gesture of kindness, but it had quickly changed to one driven by his male hormones. He wanted her, naked and willing, in his arms, a prospect which he now realised had always been in the realms of fantasy. John only had to recall the way she'd reacted to his taking her arm tonight to know he wasn't on her 'ten most desirable men in the world' list. Perhaps that was why she'd rejected his offer. That and the fact she didn't want a selfish, self-centred commitment-phobe as the father of her baby. Much better to have some anonymous stranger.

Good one, John.

A light suddenly came on in the King house. John had no idea if it was Scarlet's bedroom or not. But he suspected it was. She was sleepless, just like him.

Another memory suddenly popped into his head—that of his taking her arm when they'd left his parents' party together. Scarlet hadn't pulled away from him then. Hadn't found his touch in any way repulsive. Then there'd been the way she'd looked at him when she'd first driven up to Gosford station earlier that day. That hadn't been the look of a woman who found him unattractive.

Maybe he was reading this situation all wrong. Maybe there was something else bothering Scarlet. Maybe she had been tossing and turning in her bed over there, wishing now that she hadn't rejected his offer. Because in truth it had been a good offer, far better than her having some stranger's child. He still didn't fancy that idea one little bit.

It suddenly occurred to John that Scarlet might eventually reconsider his offer. He suspected, however, that she would not come to such a decision lightly, or in the immediate future. To hang around home, hoping for her to change her mind, was not a bearable thought. Despite his recent discovery that he still loved his father, John still found being around him difficult. He couldn't even escape by going surfing; the doctors said such activities were out of the question till his leg was stronger. He'd already told his mother when he arrived home that he was booked on a flight tomorrow evening, letting her think he was returning to Brazil, whereas in fact he was going to Darwin. She'd been disappointed by his early departure, but resigned.

Would Scarlet be disappointed by his early departure? he wondered. Or relieved.

He could hardly ask her now.

Another thought came to him. What if she *did* change her mind about his offer? She would need to know how to contact him, without having to ask his mother. No way would Scarlet do that. He knew her. She was like him in some

ways—overly proud. And too independent for
her own good.

Turning from the window, he made his way
downstairs where everything was quiet; his parents had gone to bed some time ago. Switching
on the kitchen light, he went to the drawer where
his mother kept an assortment of biros, writing
pads and different-sized envelopes. Selecting
what he wanted, he returned to his room,
switched on his bedside lamp and sat down to
write. It took him several attempts before he
got the wording just right but eventually he was
satisfied.

Dear Scarlet.
    By the time you read this I will have left.
Not Australia, as my family believe. I have
an apartment in Darwin where I go every
winter for a few weeks' rest and recreation.
This time, however, I intend to stay longer, though please keep this information
confidential. Scarlet, I presume you are
determined to keep trying for a baby by
your anonymous donor. And that is your
right. But if it is not successful, I wish you
to know that my offer is still open. I can't
promise you romance but I do promise you
what I think you need very badly. Here are

my mobile and satellite phone numbers so that you can contact me no matter where I am.

Your friend always, John.

He added the numbers then slipped the note into an envelope and wrote Scarlet's name on the front, having already decided to drop the letter into her mailbox tomorrow whilst she was at work.

By the time she got home he would be long gone.

Then it would be up to her.

CHAPTER EIGHT

Exactly one month and one day later

It HADN'T worked. Again.

Despair clutched at Scarlet's already cramping stomach as she hunched over the toilet seat. There had to be something wrong with her. Because it didn't make sense. The clinic had tried a different procedure this time, putting the sperm right into her womb instead of just on the cervix. It was a more expensive procedure but was supposed to give her a better chance of conceiving.

A total waste of money as it turned out.

She dreaded telling her mother. Yet, she would have to. Scarlet wished now that she hadn't confided her plan in the first place. She should have just gone to the clinic on her own, in secret. That way, she could have handled her disappointment in private, without the added pain of watching her mother's disappointment. Her mum sometimes pretended that she didn't mind not having grandchildren but Scarlet knew that wasn't the case. She'd often said how she'd wanted to have a bigger family herself.

Scarlet frowned at this last thought. If her mother had wanted more than one child, then why hadn't she had some more? Scarlet's Dad hadn't died till she was nine. Scarlet sucked in sharply at the possibility that her mother had been unable to conceive more babies. But if that were so, then why hadn't she mentioned it to her? It might be an important clue over why she was having such trouble conceiving herself.

Not that she could go out and ask her right now. They were both at the salon, working. Wednesday was always a busy day. It would be impossible to question her till they were on the way home late this afternoon.

Janet knew, the moment she saw Scarlet's pasty face and dull eyes, that her period had arrived. The poor darling, she thought sadly as she watched her daughter put on a smiling face for a client.

'You know, don't you, Mum?' Scarlet said the moment they were alone in the car on the way home. She'd seen the sympathy in her mother's eyes when she'd come out of the powder room a couple of hours earlier. The sympathy and the sadness.

'Yes,' was all Janet could bring herself to say. She was close to tears. Not for herself but for her daughter.

'Mum, I've been thinking, was there any physical reason why you didn't have more children?'

Janet swallowed. She'd been expecting this question for ages.

'Not that I know of,' she answered truthfully. 'I was thoroughly checked out, the same way you've been. One doctor said I wanted to fall pregnant too much. He said stress and tension can sometimes be the problem.'

'Yes, I've read about that,' Scarlet said. 'That's why couples sometimes fall pregnant after they've adopted a child.'

'Your father and I were going to adopt a child,' Janet confessed. 'But then he was...' She broke off, unable to continue.

'Oh, Mum. I'm so sorry. I know how much you loved Dad.' After the funeral, she'd listened to her mother cry at night for months and months. It never surprised Scarlet that her mother hadn't ever dated again, or remarried. She'd been a one-man woman.

Scarlet knew she'd never find that one true love like her mother had. But she was going to become a mother, come hell or high water. All afternoon, she'd been thinking about the letter

John had left for her a month ago. When she'd first read it, she'd been incredibly touched, especially with his intuitive observations about her fragile nervous state. She'd almost changed her mind about going back to the clinic and rung him straight away. But, in the end, she simply hadn't had the courage to take what would have been a really big step for her. It seemed so much simpler not to involve other people, and to not face the problem of actually having sex with John. Scarlet understood that sex for men was not the big deal it could be for women. For her, anyway. She'd become more edgy about it as she'd got older. Less confident. More...nervous.

But the time for being Nervous Nelly was long gone. If she didn't take John up on his offer she would always regret it.

Of course, *he* might have changed his mind by now. God, she hoped not!

Well, if he had, she'd just have to persuade him otherwise, Scarlet vowed with renewed resolve. If he waffled, she'd remind him how much he'd always wanted to have sex with her!

Scarlet might have been shocked at herself if she hadn't been so fired up.

'Mum, I think that I might go away for a while. On a holiday.'

'Oh? Where to?'

'Somewhere warm. In Australia, of course. I don't want to go overseas.'

'Cairns is nice at this time of year,' her mother suggested.

'I was thinking of Darwin. I've never been there. And I've always wanted to see Kakadu.' A total untruth. Scarlet had seen one or two documentaries about the Northern Territory and was not at all interested in vast wetlands filled with biting insects, wild buffalo and crocodiles.

'Really?' her mother said, sounding surprised.

'I could go on some organised tours. That way I'd have company. You could manage without me, couldn't you, Mum? Lisa would be happy to do more hours. Joanne, too.'

'Of course I could manage. I managed when you left to be an estate agent, didn't I? When were you thinking of going?'

'Not sure yet. Possibly the end of next week.' Scarlet knew exactly when she would ovulate. She'd been charting her cycle for months. Two weeks after her period started was the beginning of her peak days for conceiving. No point in going to Darwin much before then. At the same time, she had to make it seem like she was going on a real holiday. She could hardly just go for a few days.

'For how long?'

'Um. A week or so. Maybe ten days,' she added for good measure.

'So you won't be going to the clinic for another procedure next month?'

'No, Mum. I've decided to have a break from that for a while.'

Her mother actually looked relieved. 'I think that's a good idea, love. And so's this holiday. Who knows? You might meet a nice man.'

'You never know, Mum,' Scarlet said, then deftly changed the subject onto the traffic and the never-ending roadworks. She'd always been good at making conversation, but underneath her breezy chit-chat Scarlet was beginning to feel anxious about what John would say when she rang him. Which she fully intended to, at the first available moment. For if she procrastinated, her courage might falter.

As soon as they arrived home, Scarlet made the excuse that she needed to lie down for a while. When her mother offered to make her a cup of tea, she declined, saying she was going to take some pain killers and have a short nap before dinner. Fortunately, it was her mother's turn to cook. Also fortunately, Scarlet's bedroom was at the back of the house, some way from the kitchen. Once her mother turned on the television, she would not hear Scarlet talking on the phone.

Scarlet's hands were literally shaking as she drew John's letter out of the bedside drawer where she'd put it over a month ago. He'd given her two numbers, one for a regular mobile, one for a satellite phone. She sat on the side of her bed and tried the mobile number first. It rang, thank heavens. She would have hated for it to be engaged. As it was, she'd already worked herself up into a right state.

'For pity's sake, John, answer the damned thing,' she muttered under her breath after it had rung several times.

But he didn't, and the phone eventually switched to his message bank. A despairing Scarlet didn't leave any message, choosing instead to try the satellite phone first. She actually prayed as she punched in the numbers.

CHAPTER NINE

JOHN was putting a few more pieces of wood on the camp fire when he heard the distinctive ring of his satellite phone. Frowning, he crawled into his one-man tent, picked up the phone and carried it back out into the moonlight, where he stared at it briefly before sweeping the phone up to his ear.

'Hello, Scarlet,' he answered, trying to sound cool when inside he was anything but.

John had been relieved at first when she hadn't contacted him. Once he'd cleared his head, he'd told himself that it had been a crazy idea anyway. But as the days had crawled by, John's every waking moment had been haunted by the thought of going home at Christmas and seeing Scarlet with a stranger's child growing in her belly. Once again, he'd been repulsed by the idea.

After several particularly restless nights, he'd been tempted to ring her. But what could he say that he hadn't already said? It was obvious she didn't want him to father her child. To have pursued the matter would have made him look foolish.

So in the end, he'd done nothing. Literally. He hadn't tried to find work with any of the mining companies. He hadn't gone fishing, either, the way he usually did when he was holidaying in Darwin. Hadn't done a damned thing. He had just moped around the place, watching endless movies on TV and doing way too much thinking. And way too much drinking. Bianca would have said he was running away from real life. Again.

In the end, he'd had his heli-fishing mate drop him into this isolated spot for a few days and had been camping out alone. Nothing cleared the head better than communing with nature, he'd found.

And it had worked, to a degree. He'd finally begun to see the sense of Scarlet's decision not to accept his offer. Finally found some peace of mind over the situation. Or so he'd believed.

It had only taken one little phone call to shatter that illusion.

'How did you know it was me?' she asked, clearly taken aback.

'The caller ID said you were from New South

Wales,' he explained. 'You're the only person in that state who has my satellite number.'

'Oh. I see.'

John suddenly had the most appalling thought. What if she was ringing to tell him she was finally pregnant? It was possible, he supposed. She might think he would like to know.

'Why are you ringing, Scarlet?' he asked abruptly.

Scarlet's heart sank at his brusque tone.

'You've changed your mind about your offer, haven't you?' she said.

The tension in John's gut immediately melted away.

'Not at all,' he replied.

'Really?' she gasped, renewed hope flooding her heart.

'Yes, really. So what happened, Scarlet? Given the time lapse since we last spoke, I presume you went back to the clinic for another go and it didn't work.'

'I got my period today,' she confessed with a sigh.

'Like I said in my letter, my offer is open.'

Scarlet had reached the stage where she would have given anything a try. But she wasn't so desperate that she still wasn't slightly bothered by one thing. 'I know I shouldn't look a gift horse in the mouth, John, but I still can't work out why you're doing this for me. Aside from the sex angle, that is. Which I also still can't fathom. I mean, if you always fancied me, then why didn't you do something about it before this?'

They were logical questions, John accepted. He wished he had some logical answers for her. He had to tell her something, he supposed, something which would satisfy her intelligence. Scarlet was no dummy.

'Can I be blunt with you?' he said.

'Please do.'

'I didn't do anything before this because I thought you would just knock me back,' he said, not untruthfully. 'Until we met again last month and I realised that the attraction was mutual. However, contrary to your belief, I also like you a lot, Scarlet, and I want to help you get what you obviously want very much—which is a baby. And, as strange as it seems, I also quite like the idea of having a child of my own. But if I'm to be brutally honest, what I want most is you, in my bed, for a good deal longer than you spend at that wretched clinic each month.'

Scarlet's silence at the other end of the line indicated a degree of shock. Or deep thoughtfulness. John suspected the former. He had gone overboard a bit in his attempt to focus on the sex angle. But he didn't want her questioning him further over his motives. He didn't understand them fully himself! All he knew was that his blood was racing through his body with a surge of entirely male, powerful satisfaction at her agreement. For a short time, Scarlet was going to be his.

Scarlet had been rendered speechless by the decidedly R-rated images which had sprung into her mind. She was seriously glad that John couldn't see the burst of heat which flamed into her cheeks.

'Come now, Scarlet, you must know how very desirable you are.'

Now Scarlet felt hot all over. A shiver ran down her spine at the realisation she might shortly find out just how desirable he thought she was.

'I hope your silence doesn't mean you've changed your mind about this?' he said, his voice sounding curiously expressionless.

'No,' she choked out, still blushing at her earlier train of thought. Thank heavens they weren't face to face!

'Good.' His voice relaxed again. 'When can you get yourself up here?'

Scarlet swallowed, then sat up straighter.

She'd always been more comfortable following a plan.

'I thought as soon as possible,' she said briskly.

'How about the beginning of next week?'

'Well, I'll have to get stuff organised at work...'

He rode over her objections. 'I'm sure you can sort it. Once you've booked your flight next week, text me your time of arrival and I'll be at the airport waiting for you.' He sounded equally brisk, and it was as difficult as ever to guess what he was feeling. 'Don't send the text to this number. Send it to my mobile. I'll be back in Darwin by then.'

Scarlet rolled her eyes in exasperation. Why was it then men wouldn't *listen*? 'Where are you, anyway?' she asked.

'Camping out in one of the national parks.'

Scarlet had been doing some mental calculations. 'Wait—next week is way too early. I can't possibly fall pregnant till a week after that. I never ovulate before day fourteen on my cycle. I know this for a fact because I've been taking my temperature every day for the last year and—'

'Scarlet,' he interrupted. 'If you want to get pregnant, then let's try this *my* way.'

Truly, he could be as irritating a man as he'd been an irritating boy! 'Which is?' she snapped.

'Not taking your temperature every day, for

starters. Not caring about when you bloody ovulate either. Because, let's face it, that method hasn't been working too well for you up till now, has it?'

'I guess not,' she admitted grudgingly.

'I suggest you leave this whole operation up to me. Put yourself entirely in my hands. No arguments, no more buts.'

'Yes,' she bit out.

'Good,' he said, smiling wryly to himself at the thought that 'yes' wasn't a word Scarlet was used to saying. But she was going to say it a lot during their time together. He would *make* her say it. No, he would make her *want* to say it. For that was what he craved all of a sudden. Not just Scarlet's compliance but her complete surrender.

The thought excited him unbearably. Was this what had been lurking at the back of his mind? Not just desire for sex, but a desire to seduce? To possess? To control?

The idea perturbed him. He'd never been into that kind of thing. Sex for him was usually just a physical release with no strings attached. He'd always steered well clear of becoming emotionally involved with the women he slept with. John could see, however, that this was a different situation entirely. If truth be told, his emotions were already involved. The problem was which ones?

He almost told her to forget it then; that *he'd*

changed his mind. But it was too late. The roller coaster of destiny was already moving and he was solidly strapped in. There would be no escape till it came to rest at the end of the ride.

CHAPTER TEN

BECAUSE she had a window seat and her head was too fuzzy to read, Scarlet spent most of the four-and-a-half-hour flight to Darwin staring down at the landscape below. With no clouds in the sky, there was nothing to hinder her view of what was really an incredible sight. What a big country Australia was, big and rugged and mostly uninhabited. The last frontier, some people called it.

Scarlet had never flown over the outback of Australia before. Or *been* in the outback, for that matter. Holidays before her dad had died had been confined to trips to Sydney, or the Gold Coast. Once, they'd gone to the Blue Mountains where they'd visited the Three Sisters and the Jenolan Caves. After her dad had died, she and her mother hadn't gone on holidays for years. Eventually, they had started going to Fiji each year, because it was reasonably close to Australia and good value for money.

She'd never been to Darwin. But she knew quite a bit about the place. Or she did now, having looked it up on the Internet this past week. Scarlet was not a girl who ever liked to appear ignorant. Up till now her knowledge of the capital city of the Northern Territory had been rather superficial and sketchy. Although she already knew that Darwin had been struck by a cyclone in the seventies, she hadn't realised it had happened on Christmas Day, of all days, which she found very sad. She also hadn't appreciated the devastation it had caused. The photographs of the aftermath had been horrendous. Understandably, it had taken decades to rebuild the city but it was now a thriving mining town and tourist Mecca, the gateway to Kakadu National Park and lots of other famous Aboriginal sites. Its harbourside position in the extreme north of Australia meant its climate was very hot and humid in the summer, but wonderfully mild in the winter.

She'd dithered considerably over what to bring, in the end packing probably more than she would need. But it had been so hard to choose. Scarlet had always loved nice clothes, and had a wardrobe full of outfits for every occasion. Her mother had thought she was crazy putting in a couple of pretty dresses, but that was because she believed Scarlet was going to spend her 'holiday' either lazing around the pool of the hotel she'd supposedly booked, or going on day bus-tours, all of which required nothing more than Bermuda shorts, solid shoes, a hat and insect repellent. Her mother had stopped criticising her choice of wardrobe when Scarlet reminded her about that nice man she might meet.

'Who knows?' she'd added for good measure. 'He might ask me out to dinner!'

Which she'd assumed John would at some stage.

But what if he didn't? Scarlet now wondered.

During the past week, Scarlet had tried not to think about what John's plans were for the next ten days. For what was the point? She'd already agreed to his terms, whatever they were.

But, now that the moment was at hand, it was almost impossible not to wonder, and worry. Maybe she should have warned him that she was a bit of a lemon in the bedroom. It was one thing to have private fantasies where she stripped off without a qualm and had multiple orgasms every single time she had sex. The reality was totally different. She was rather shy at being naked in front of a man.

Her stomach tightened as she tried to imagine what it was going to be like, having sex with John. For some crazy reason she was terrified of disappointing him. She wanted him to find pleasure in her body.

The announcement that they'd begun their descent into Darwin tightened her stomach further. If Scarlet hadn't been so besieged by nervous tension, she might have noticed that she'd stopped thinking about what she'd come to Darwin to achieve. All her thoughts were on one subject and one subject only: John.

Seeking distraction, she stared once more at the ground below, surprised to see that the red and brown of the outback had given way to a greener landscape, one with lots of trees and, yes, water out to the left of the plane. It looked like a harbour but obviously not Darwin harbour. There were no houses along the foreshore and not many boats on the water. Of course, it always took a good while for a commercial jet to descend into an airport, so they weren't over Darwin yet.

When the plane banked sharply, the setting sun shone straight into Scarlet's eyes. She automatically shut them, then kept them shut, always having found landing stressful, though this time her stresses were many and varied.

The landing seemed to take for ever, but exiting the plane was relatively quick, thank goodness, as her seat was right down the back, not far from the exit. She walked across the tarmac towards the terminal building, her only thought at that moment being that every step brought her closer to John.

John stood at a window in the arrivals area, scanning the passengers as they left the plane. He spotted Scarlet immediately, the rays of the setting sun bouncing gold off her blonde hair which was down and blowing in the breeze. She was wearing jeans and a white jacket, with a white-and-blue top underneath. She looked utterly gorgeous, sexy and…very tense. Her forehead was scrunched into a frown and her walk was fast and anxious, passing several other passengers before entering the terminal building.

Clearly, she didn't see him standing nearby, although her eyes were darting around the place. When he stepped forward to make his presence known, she gave him a tight smile, obviously very nervous indeed. At her request, he led her to the nearest ladies' room, waiting patiently outside for her return, using the time to gather his thoughts and assess his reaction to her arrival.

There was only one word to describe the way he was feeling.

Excited. More excited than he'd been in years. Not just sexual excitement, though that was there as well. Hell, yes! He'd had a hard-on for days. But there was another excitement firing him up: the excitement which came from rising to meet a challenge.

During the last week or so John had given a lot of thought to why he was doing this. He'd finally come to the conclusion that it was his male ego that had directed his offer to Scarlet. There wasn't anything mysterious or confusing about it. It was his competitive spirit coming to the fore. He, John Mitchell, was going to do what no other man could do. His intense desire to give Scarlet a baby wasn't just sexual, it was *primal*. Man doing what he was put on earth to do: propagate.

Scarlet had been spot on when she'd said having a child was a basic drive for men as well as for women. It was.

All these realisations had led John to approach his time with Scarlet as much more than an opportunistic affair. It was an important project, to be researched and carried out with meticulous attention to detail. When he'd been looking for oil in Argentina he hadn't just lucked upon the discovery. It had taken months of painstaking work, both physical and intellectual. So he'd set about researching the reasons for an otherwise healthy woman not conceiving with the same dogged determination. After reading every article on the Internet on the subject, he'd come to the conclusion that Scarlet's most likely problem was stress, something he'd already suspected.

She needed to relax more and stop obsessing about having a baby.

Which was where he came in. His job was to relax her, and the best way to relax her was through sex. Not just ordinary old sex—great sex. The kind which would eventually make the woman forget everything but having her partner deep inside her. John had concluded that Mother Nature had created orgasms for a reason, so making sure that Scarlet had fun was his number one priority.

Luckily, John knew his way around a woman's body very well indeed. Knew what pleasured them. Knew what was likely to satisfy them. Scarlet had obviously had some negative experiences where the opposite sex was concerned. It made sense that she'd been turned off men to a degree.

She'd probably expect him to make a pass tonight. All the more reason why he wouldn't. Let her be impressed with his gentlemanly manners and his apartment. It was a very nice apartment. He'd give her one of the two guest rooms, the one which opened out onto the balcony with a view of the harbour, the same balcony his bedroom opened onto. Tomorrow, he would take her sightseeing during the day, wine and dine her in the evening, then make love to her afterwards. Romantic sex, the kind with silk sheets and candles.

John's mouth quirked. Unfortunately, he didn't have silk sheets or candles. He wasn't that kind of guy. Damn. Still, perhaps it was for the best not to get too romantic—it might...confuse the issue.

Such thinking brought a rueful laugh to his lips. Scarlet King, fall in love with *him*? Not bloody likely!

Scarlet felt marginally better by the time she emerged from the ladies' room. Besides a much-needed trip to the loo, she'd taken off her jacket and brushed her hair. But the sight of John standing there brought a swarm of butterflies to her stomach. She still couldn't get used to how sexy she found him. He looked very attractive, dressed in fawn cargo shorts and a white polo shirt which highlighted his tan, as well as his broad-shouldered, very fit body.

She also couldn't get used to the way he kept looking at her, like she was a freshly cooked pizza and he a starving Italian. His obvious desire was both flattering and nerve-wracking at the same time. Her pulse-rate definitely moved up several notches.

Scooping in a deep breath, she hooked her bag over her right shoulder, draped her jacket over her left arm and moved towards him, fiercely aware of the movements slow walking and fast breathing were creating in her female body. The soft rise and fall of her breasts. The sway of her hips. Lord, but she was blushing now!

Thankfully, his eyes had by then moved in the direction of the nearby carousel where the luggage was coming out.

'What does your bag look like?' he asked, glancing back over his shoulder at her.

'It's black with a big pink ribbon tied to the handle. There it is now,' she said, pointing.

John strode over and scooped her bag off the carousel, his eyebrows lifting when he felt the weight of it. 'I only asked you to come for ten days, Scarlet,' he said with dry amusement as he steered her towards the exit, dragging the bag behind them. 'Not for life.'

'I hate going away anywhere and getting caught with either not enough clothes or all the wrong ones.'

'Can't say it's a problem I have often.'

'You're not a female.'

'Which is rather a good thing,' he said with a wry little smile.

Scarlet ground to a halt and stared up at him.

'What?' he said.

'Do I know you at all, John Mitchell? I thought I did. I thought I had you pegged as that introverted, antisocial pain-in-the-neck kid from across the street who'd grown up into an irritatingly gorgeous but pain-in-the-neck adult. Instead, suddenly, I find out you're nothing like that at all. You're actually quite witty and charming and…and…'

'Maybe you never knew the real John Mitchell,' he countered.

'Obviously I didn't. What other surprises do you have in store for me?'

'Shall we go and find out?' he said, taking her elbow again and leading her out to the visitors' car-park.

His SUV didn't surprise her, despite being relatively new and relatively unused. But the sheet of paper waiting on the passenger seat did. It was the printout of a medical bill of health.

She shook her head from side to side as she read it. 'It was very thoughtful of you to do this, John,' she said.

'I just didn't want to you to worry about anything at any stage. I wasn't going to offer you less than what you were getting at that clinic. I'm quite sure your anonymous donor had a similar clearance.'

'Yes. Yes, he did,' she said, frowning. 'I should have thought to ask you, but I didn't. It was silly of me.'

'Not silly. Just human. You've been upset

lately. And very busy. But you would have thought of it eventually, and you would have worried. Now, you don't have to.'

'No,' she said, and smiled over at him. 'I don't. Thank you again, John. For everything.'

'Don't start canonising me yet, Scarlet.'

'I see,' she said, and gave him a much more typical Scarlet look. Very droll. 'I'll try not to jump to saintly conclusions about you in future.'

'That would be wise.'

By the time they left the airport, the sun had set and night was only a few minutes away. Despite the roads into the city being well lit, it wasn't easy for a newcomer to Darwin to see much during the short drive to the city, so John didn't bother doing the tourist-guide bit of pointing things out to her. Scarlet did remark on how good the road was. John explained that most of the infrastructure was fairly new and well planned, one positive legacy of the cyclone. In just over ten minutes, they were entering the Central Business District which naturally, was a lot smaller than Sydney's.

'It all looks very neat and tidy,' Scarlet commented as he drove up Stuart Street then turned left into the Esplanade which was one of the best streets in Darwin to live in, in John's opinion. As well as being right on top of the CBD, it was facing the water in a south-westerly direction which meant you could still see the magnificent sunsets as well as get the advantage of the sea breezes.

His apartment was towards the southerly end of the street in a multi-storeyed building whose walls were cement rendered in an attractive grey-blue colour. There were lots of balconies facing the water, all of them enclosed with glass panels and black railings. The gutterings, trim and window frames were all black which looked extremely smart indeed. The garages were in the basement, with John having two allotted spaces for himself and guests. He parked in one, then helped Scarlet out before removing her bag from the back. She didn't say a word as he led her over to the lift. Maybe she was worrying that he would pounce the moment they were alone.

Her head whipped round to stare at him when he pressed the top floor button.

'You live in a penthouse?' she asked, taken aback.

'Not exactly. Penthouses usually occupy the whole top floor. There are two top-floor apartments of equal size, one of which is mine.'

She fell silent once more till John showed her into the apartment, at which point she stared at him again, shaking her head at the same time. 'You really are very rich, aren't you?'

'Rich enough.'

'For what?'

He shrugged. 'I don't have to work for the rest of my life if I don't want to. Though of course I will.'

Again she shook her head. 'This place must have cost a small fortune.'

'Not quite that much. I bought it off-plan a few years ago.'

'Did you choose the furniture?'

'Lord, no. I have absolutely no taste whatever in that regard. I had it professionally decorated and furnished. Would you like to see the rest of it?'

'Yes, please.'

Scarlet quickly noted that the same colour palate had been used throughout the whole apartment, ranging from white, to white with a greyish tinge, to various shades of grey right through to black, splashes of turquoise brightening up what could otherwise have been a dull decor. Which no doubt was why the designer had chosen glass surfaces for the various tables in the living area, to lift the heaviness of the black leather sofas and chairs.

Scarlet loved the circular glass dining table—which was set in a hexagonal-shaped alcove—and had a large turquoise ceramic bowl sitting in the middle. She even loved the dining chairs, which were black leather on chrome frames. The kitchen was spectacular, the stainless steel appliances and turquoise splashback set off beautifully by black cupboard doors and white stone benchtops which had grey flecks in it. The three chrome-based stools which were tucked neatly under the breakfast bar had turquoise leather saddle-seats which had to have been specially made.

The two guest bedrooms were similarly sized and furnished, with queen-sized beds, white lacquered furniture and white shag rugs on the floor, though the bed linen was different. One had a rather masculine black, grey and white striped quilt set whereas the second one was more feminine, a white background with turquoise flowers on it. That bedroom also opened out onto the front balcony, unlike the other one. The main bathroom, situated between the two guest bedrooms, was all white with silver taps and trim, and the loveliest, thickest turquoise towels. Scarlet was rather particular when it came to bathrooms and could find no fault anywhere in that one.

When she commented on how spotless everything was, John informed her that he had the apartment serviced every few days when he was in town.

'Housekeeping,' he added, 'is not my forte.'

Scarlet didn't imagine that it would be. He was

a man's man, with an outdoors job and outdoors hobbies such as surfing and camping.

The last room John showed her was the master bedroom, which blew her away even more than the kitchen. The black quilt on the king-sized bed contrasted beautifully with the white lacquered bedhead and side tables. The bedside lamps were exquisite, with chrome bases and exotic black shades which had crystal drops hanging from the bottom edges. Two rectangular white shag rugs were perfectly positioned on either side of the bed and a huge flat-screen television was built into the wall opposite the foot of the bed.

Scarlet suddenly saw herself sitting stark naked in that decadent-looking bed, propped up against a mountain of pillows whilst John was doing unimaginable things to her. It was a struggle not to blush once again—something which she seemed to be doing a lot in John's presence. Somehow, she made some innocuous compliment and took refuge by thoroughly inspecting the oversized walk-in wardrobe, before moving onto the black marble *en suite* bathroom where everything seemed to have been built for two. A spa bath *and* a shower. She couldn't look at either without once again picturing herself in there, naked again of course, with an equally naked John doing even more unimaginable things to her. And not under any covers.

Once again, heat zoomed into her cheeks.

Thankfully, her back was to John.

'You've gone rather quiet,' he said from just behind her. 'Is there something wrong?'

By the time she turned around, Scarlet had her blushing under control. She even managed a polite smile. 'Not at all. This place is lovely, John.'

'But...?'

'But what?'

'I was sure I heard a "but" in there somewhere.'

Scarlet decided to take the bull by the horns in an attempt to defuse the nervous tension which was building up inside her. 'I was wondering if you expected me to join you in here tonight.'

In spite of his earlier plans, John was tempted to say *yes, by God, of course I am*. But he could see that she wasn't ready. She was way too tense for him to achieve what he wanted to achieve, which wasn't just satisfaction for himself but satisfaction for her.

'I thought you'd be too tired,' he said, doing his best to ignore his body, which shouted in protest.

She smiled. A rather odd smile, but a smile nevertheless.

'When I'm nervous about something, I like to get it over and done with as soon as possible.'

'There's no reason for you to be nervous.'

Scarlet laughed. 'You have no idea.'

'I have no idea about what?'

Her face twisted into a grimace. 'I should have told you earlier.'

'Told me what?'

'I think I might be a little bit frigid.'

John's surprise must have shown in his eyes, for Scarlet looked away from him. 'This is so embarrassing,' she choked out.

He deliberated for a moment, then reached out to take gentle possession of her chin and turn her face back to his. He doubted very much that she was frigid—he'd seen passion in her too many times.

'Let's just take this one step at a time,' he said softly, his eyes holding hers. 'You like to be kissed, don't you? When you're with a man you're attracted to, that is.'

She blinked, then nodded.

Scarlet thought he was going to kiss her. But he didn't. Instead, he released her chin then lifted his hand to rub two of his fingertips back and forth along her lower lip, before tracing the full circle of her mouth over and over. Soon, her lips were tingling, her heart was pounding madly in her chest and she was *dying* for him to kiss her. Her mouth fell open as she struggled for breath, her tongue drying as she sucked in much-needed air. At which point he finally did what she craved: removed his fingers and replaced them with his lips.

It was a kiss such as she had never experienced before. Perversely restrained, but incredibly exciting. He cupped her face as he gently caressed her swollen lips, till a frustrated moan escaped her throat. Only then did he deepen the kiss, his lips applying more pressure, holding her lips far enough apart for his tongue to slide into her mouth.

Scarlet's head whirled. She could not think straight. Neither did she care. All she wanted was for John to keep on kissing her.

But he didn't.

She made some sort of protest when his mouth lifted abruptly from hers. A moan. A groan. She could not be sure which.

When she stared up at John she saw that he didn't seem at all rattled.

'I take it then,' he said coolly, 'that you find me attractive?'

Her stare became a glare. 'You're an arrogant bastard, John Mitchell.'

His smile widened. 'And you're incredibly beautiful, Scarlet King.'

She pursed her lips in defiance at the involuntary pleasure his compliment gave her.

'You're also not even a little bit frigid.'

'Oh!' she exclaimed frustratedly. 'You really are the most annoying man.'

'But an attractive one,' he reminded her with a perfectly straight face.

She couldn't help it. She laughed. 'Whatever am I going to do with you?' she said without thinking.

John's eyebrows arched, his eyes twinkling suggestively.

Scarlet's own blue eyes narrowed. 'Don't you dare say another thing. Now, I'm going to go unpack in one of the guest bedrooms. I'd love the one with the turquoise flowers, if it's okay with you? Meanwhile, I don't suppose there's any food about?'

'Unfortunately, cooking is not my forte either,' he returned. 'So the best I can offer you is take-away for tonight. But I know lots of local Asian-style restaurants who'll deliver within half an hour. What would you prefer? Chinese? Thai? Vietnamese?'

'I'm not fussy,' she said. 'You choose.'

'Thai it is, then,' he said as they both turned and walked back into the living room. 'Join me back in here when you're ready. I bought some snacks and some wine in anticipation of your visit.'

Scarlet almost told him that she didn't usually drink much; that she'd just been upset that day. But she didn't want to bring up the subject of her ongoing failure to conceive a child. For a while there, she'd forgotten about that. She'd forgotten to ring her mother as well. Oh dear.

'I'll have to ring my mother first before I do another thing,' she said, feeling terribly guilty. 'Let her know I've arrived safely.'

'Fine. You do that. I'll go ring the restaurant. And Scarlet…?'

'What?'

'You can relax; I promise I won't be making you to do anything you don't want to.' His mouth curled up in a wicked smile. 'Not unless you beg me, anyway.'

CHAPTER ELEVEN

A WORRIED Janet King jumped to answer the phone as soon as it rang, relief flooding through her when she saw it was her daughter's mobile number on the display. She'd always hated flying and had been tense all afternoon at the salon, especially when the estimated time of arrival of Scarlet's flight had come and gone without a call. She'd been glad to come home where she didn't have to make polite conversation and where she could show her agitation by grumbling at the news reader on the television. Her nerve-endings were still strung out as she swept the receiver up to her ear.

'Hi, Mum,' Scarlet said before she could utter a word. 'You can relax now. The plane didn't crash and I'm safely at the hotel.'

'I wish you'd rung me from the airport,' Janet said plaintively. 'I've been worried sick.' The words were barely out of her mouth when she regretted them. She hated mothers who talked like that to their adult children. It put them in a terrible position.

Scarlet smothered a sigh. 'Sorry. I thought I'd wait till I got to the hotel so that I could tell you about it.'

'I'm the one who's sorry, darling. You've gone up there for a rest and here I am, putting guilt trips on you already. I promise not to keep on being a pain. Or to expect you to ring me all the time. But, yes, I would like to know about the hotel. Is your room nice?'

Scarlet moved over to sit on one of the huge black leather sofas, amazed at how soft and comfortable it was. 'Very,' she said as she leant back into its squashy depths. 'Has all the mod cons and a view of the harbour.'

'You never did tell me how much you paid for it.'

Scarlet winced at the lies she'd told, both directly and by omission. She hadn't realised how awkward things could become. 'Actually, I didn't just book a room, Mum. It's an apartment.'

'Goodness! It's not like you to be so extravagant, Scarlet, except perhaps when it comes to clothes. Not that I'm complaining, mind. You deserve some spoiling after all you've been through.'

It was ironic that, right at that moment, John came into the living room carrying a frosted glass of white wine which he handed to Scarlet, who mouthed, "Thank you," before lifting the glass to her lips. She had a feeling she was going to need a drink or two before this night was out.

'You'll have to send me some photos of the place,' her mother added.

Scarlet took a sip of the deliciously chilled wine whilst wondering how she could avoid doing that. Perhaps she could just send photos of the view, the guest bedroom, half the main bathroom and about a quarter of the humungous kitchen. But not right now.

'Can I leave that till tomorrow morning, Mum? I'm pretty bushed tonight. I just want to have a shower and go straight to bed.'

'Without eating anything?'

'I won't starve, Mum. There's a small stock of essentials in the kitchen,' she said truthfully. John had shown her the floor-to-ceiling pantry. 'It's lovely. There's even a complimentary bottle of very good white wine in the fridge.' She raised her glass in a toast-like gesture to John who'd settled himself on the sofa adjacent to hers. He smiled back whilst stretching his long arms along the back of the sofa, looking ridiculously sexy.

A distracting thought. It reminded her of an explicit image she'd briefly entertained last week. It was difficult for her mind not to dwell on her fantasy, when she would soon become extremely intimate with the real thing.

Though not tonight…

Was she really relieved about that?

Scarlet could not deny that, whilst she was still nervous about going to bed with John, she no longer felt afraid of it. Perversely, she was almost looking forward to it. A man who kissed as well and as imaginatively as he did would surely be a good lover. Gosh, he really did have a great body.

When she felt in danger of ogling him again, Scarlet reefed her eyes away and focused firmly on her conversation with her mother.

'So how did you cope today without me?' she asked.

'Fine. Though none of the other girls are a patch on you when it comes to colour. I suspect a few of your clients will wait till you come back before getting theirs done again. Still, you'll only be gone ten days. It's not an eternity. I'm sure they'll survive.'

'I'm sure they will. I'd better go now, Mum. I keep on yawning. I'll give you a call again tomorrow night.'

'I'd like that. You can tell me what you've been up to all day.'

Scarlet swallowed, then glanced over at John. Would he want to make love in the morning, in broad daylight? Or would he wait till tomorrow night?

'I...er... I doubt I'll be doing too much tomorrow,' she said. 'I might just walk around the city and get my bearings. Do a little shopping for food. I don't fancy going out to restaurants on my own so I'll probably cook.'

'Sounds nice. Night night, darling. Love you.'

'Love you too, Mum. Bye.' After she hung up, Scarlet took a deep swallow of the wine before glancing over at John.

'Mothers!' she said with a mixture of exasperation and affection.

'They mean well,' he replied.

'But?' Scarlet prompted with a wry little smile. 'I'm sure I heard a but in there somewhere,' she added, echoing the words he'd used earlier.

His smile carried amusement. 'I think you're the witty one here, Scarlet, not me. But, no, no buts. Mothers will be mothers, no matter how old their children get. You just have to learn how to circumnavigate their tendency to cling and control without their knowing how much you hate it.'

'But I don't hate it,' she said. 'Not the way you do. I think of my mother's concern for me as caring, not clinging and controlling.'

He shrugged his shoulders. 'Not all mothers

are equal. Yours, I have to admit, is especially nice.'

'So is yours.'

'True. But mine is married to my father.'

Scarlet tipped her head slightly to one side as she searched his face. 'I've always wanted to ask you why you hate your father so much. I mean… I know he's not the happiest of souls but he's still your father.'

'Please don't go down that road, Scarlet.'

'What road?'

'The third degree road.'

'I was just curious about the relationship between you and your father. I have no intention of asking you a whole heap of questions about your life.'

'Good. Because I have no intention of answering them,' he growled as he crossed his arms in a belligerent fashion.

Scarlet added 'defensive' and 'secretive' to John's list of personality flaws, along with arrogant and rude.

'Charming,' she muttered.

'No. I'm actually not at all charming,' he admitted drily. 'I'm exactly what you called me earlier—introverted and antisocial.'

Scarlet's blood pressure began to rise. 'For pity's sake, let's not go down that road, either!'

'And what road is *that*, might I ask?' he snapped.

'The back-to-the-future childish road, where we fight all the time and end up spoiling what I came up here for. Trust me when I say I no longer wish to know the ins and out of your life story. I know I originally said I did but I've changed my mind on that score. I don't give a damn where you've been all these years, what you've done or who you've slept with, safely or otherwise. I also don't give a damn how bloody rich you are. All I care about is whether this works and we can actually make a baby!'

She was still glaring at him several seconds later when the beginnings of a smile tugged at the corners of his tightly pressed lips. Before long he was smiling broadly at her.

'You always were good at tongue lashings.'

Scarlet refused to smile back at him. She was still way too angry. Instead, she took another gulp of wine. When it went straight to her head, she realised she really needed to eat something. And soon.

As if on cue, the buzzer to the apartment's security system went off, indicating that someone required entry to the building. Hopefully, it was someone delivering the Thai food.

'Saved by the bell,' John quipped and stood up. 'That should be dinner,' he said as he walked to the front door where he flipped a switch on the wall console and asked who it was.

'Dinner delivery for John Mitchell.'

'I'll come down and get it.'

Scarlet sat and worried a little about the future while he was downstairs, then decided she had to stop thinking. She drained her glass, then went out to the kitchen where she refilled from the opened wine bottle she found in the fridge door and returned to sit, sipping in silence, as she waited for John's return.

He arrived with some delicious-smelling containers.

'Let's go eat this in the kitchen. Unless of course you want me to set the dining table?' he added.

'I don't think we have time for that,' Scarlet said when she stood up and the room spun round. 'If I don't eat something in the next five minutes, I'm going to become seriously tipsy.'

'On one glass of wine?'

'I refilled whilst you were downstairs.'

'You drunkard, you!'

'Stop mocking me and go serve up that food!'

'Can you make it to the kitchen on your own or do you want me to carry you?'

She rolled her eyes at him. 'I think I can make it that far alone.'

'What a shame. I've always wanted to sweep you up into my arms.'

'You liar, you!'

He sighed melodramatically. 'Oh, Scarlet, whatever am I going to do with you?'

'Hopefully, you're going to feed me.'

CHAPTER TWELVE

JOHN was still sitting up in his bed, watching television, at eleven-fifteen. It was a deep-sea fishing documentary which would normally have interested him. But his mind kept wandering. The only reason he had the TV on was that he couldn't sleep. He couldn't stop thinking about Scarlet.

He now regretted his decision to leave making love to Scarlet till tomorrow. His desire had deepened with each minute he spent with her. Even when she was being sassy or actively rude, he wanted her. Actually, the sassier she was, the *more* he wanted her. It was all rather perverse. He could not wait till the morning. Yet he would have to, he supposed. He could hardly barge into her bedroom at this late hour and demand she honour their deal, particularly when she was fast asleep. That would hardly endear him to her. Which would be a shame, considering they were getting along surprisingly well, despite the sarcastic repartee which they both seemed compelled to indulge in. But what the hell? He'd enjoyed it.

Unfortunately, the evening had ended shortly after the meal was over, with Scarlet claiming total exhaustion.

He'd listened to her in the shower as he'd cleaned up the kitchen, his mind bombarded with the image of her standing there naked whilst jets of hot water streamed over her shoulders and back. Before long the image had become a fully fledged sexual fantasy. In his head she'd turned around so that the water splashed over her face and threw her head back, arching her spine so that her breasts were thrust up towards the water, gasping when it beat against her erect nipples, her belly quivering with anticipation.

Because of course in this fantasy she hadn't been alone. He'd been there in the shower, close behind her, watching and waiting. But not for long. Soon, she'd handed him a cake of soap and asked him to wash her. Which he had, oh so slowly, all over. It was deliciously decadent, the way she'd moaned. And the way she'd moved, parting her legs and inviting him in.

Unfortunately, she'd switched the shower off at that point, leaving him so damned frustrated that he could have screamed. He'd quickly headed for a shower himself, a cold one, where shards of icy water had lashed his overheated body till it was devoid of desire. But it was only a temporary solution. By the time he'd dried himself and climbed into bed shortly after eight-thirty, John had briefly contemplated doing something about the situation himself but abandoned that idea when he remembered that too much ejaculation lowered a man's sperm count. After all, Scarlet was depending on him.

No, not him especially, John reminded himself when he found himself feeling smug over this idea. Just about anyone would do. *No point in pretending you're anything special to Scarlet.*

It was perverse that this fact irked him. Male egos had a lot to answer for, John decided.

The sudden knock on his bedroom door had his heart almost jumping out of his chest. Which was ridiculous, for it could only be Scarlet.

'Come in,' he called out. 'I'm still awake,' he added somewhat unnecessarily. She could obviously see light under his door and hear the television on, otherwise she wouldn't have knocked. For a split second, John indulged in a new fantasy, one where she hadn't been able to sleep and had come to seduce him dressed in a provocative negligee.

It was a fantasy soon dashed when she opened the door and stood there in the most unprovocative nightwear he'd ever seen. Not that the pink polka-dotted shortie pyjamas she was wearing were unattractive. They were quite cute, but in the night light, with her face scrubbed clean of make-up and her hair up in a pony-tail, Scarlet looked as she'd looked when she'd been sixteen.

He'd found her indescribably sexy when she'd been sixteen. His own sixteen-year-old hormones had been raging. He'd been secretly dying to go to her sixteenth birthday party; had even planned to be nice to her. But an invitation had never arrived for him. She hadn't wanted him then and she didn't really want him now. He was just a means to an end.

'Sorry to bother you, John,' she said as she stood there, looking somewhat embarrassed. 'But I've woken up with this most awful headache. I looked in all the cupboards in the bathroom and kitchen for some pain killers but couldn't find any.'

'Really? I thought I put some headache pills in the cupboard above the fridge.'

'Oh, I didn't look in that one. It was too high up.'

'Never mind, I have some in my bathroom cupboard. I'll just go get them for you.'

Scarlet stiffened when he threw back his bed covers, suddenly afraid that he was naked. He'd *looked* naked, sitting there, propped up against a mountain of pillows, his chest totally bare right down to his waistline. But he was actually wearing a pair of black satin boxer shorts, slung low on his hips.

'What do you want?' he threw over his shoulder as he padded across the rug towards the bathroom. 'Paracetemol, or something stronger?'

'Nothing with codeine in it,' she replied. 'That makes me feel sick.'

'Paracetemol it is, then.' He returned a minute later with two tablets in one hand and a glass of water in the other. 'Drink all the water,' he advised as he handed both over to her. 'The flight and the alcohol have probably left you dehydrated.'

Scarlet did as she was told, gazing up at the television on the wall whilst she gulped down the water. It was better than ogling John, though he was well worth ogling. He really did have a great body—broad at the shoulder and slim at the hips, with a washboard stomach and just enough muscle in his arms and legs to look strongly masculine without being muscle bound. He wasn't overly hairy either, but there was a nice sprinkling of dark curls in the middle of his tanned chest—a chest which Scarlet wouldn't mind running her hands over. That was a startling thought for a girl who'd never taken the initiative in love-making in her entire life.

'Thank you,' she said when she handed the

empty glass back to him. 'Sorry to have bothered you.'

'No bother. No, don't go,' he said abruptly when she turned to leave. 'Stay and watch TV with me till your headache goes.'

Scarlet had to admit that she was tempted. The thought of going back to the guest bedroom, alone, was not appealing. She suspected she might find it hard to go back to sleep, not because of the headache but because of the agitating thoughts which kept running through her head. Thoughts of John and sex. She turned back to face him, then glanced at the TV. 'Could we watch something else rather than fishing?'

'Absolutely. You can have control of the remote. There are loads of channels to choose from.'

'But where will I sit?' There was a two-seater lounger against one wall but it was under the television.

'In bed next to me, of course,' he said.

She stared at him, knowing full well what would eventually happen if she climbed into that bed.

'I promise I won't touch you, Scarlet,' he said, his eyes locking with hers. 'Not unless you want me to.'

Scarlet shook her head slowly from side to side. 'I don't know what I want any more.'

'That's because you over-think everything. Time to just let nature takes its course. You find me attractive, don't you?'

Her eyes swept over his near-naked body once more. 'Yes,' she choked out.

'And you enjoyed my kissing you earlier?'

'Yes,' she agreed again.

'How's the headache now?'

'What? Oh, er, not as bad, actually.'

'Ten more minutes and you'll feel much better, especially if you lie down in my very comfy bed and let me stroke your hair.'

'Stroke my hair,' she repeated numbly, an erotic quiver running down her spine.

'You'll have to take it down out of that ponytail of course,' he said. 'Here, I'll do it for you.'

He moved behind her, his hands swift and sure as they removed the rubber band, letting her hair tumble free over her shoulders.

'This way,' he said, and led her over to the bed where he threw back the covers before suddenly whirling and scooping her up into his arms.

Scarlet gasped in shock, both at the speed of his actions and the way it felt, being held hard against his naked chest. Her arms automatically lifted to wind themselves around his neck, her eyes blinking wide as they met his.

'Like I said earlier,' he said wryly. 'I've always wanted to sweep you off your feet. Now, don't say anything sarcastic, Scarlet. I know you're itching to. I can see it in your face. But this is not the time for one-upmanship. It's time for you to just trust me.'

As surprising as it was, she *did* trust him, almost as much as she desired him. It was a strange situation, one which brought a puzzled frown to her face, until she winced as a new wave of pain hit her.

'That headache is still bothering you, isn't it?' he said sympathetically as he lowered her onto the bed, her head and shoulders sinking into the layers of black pillows propped against the bedhead.

'I think, under the circumstances,' he added as he strode round the other side of the bed and climbed in next to her, 'that watching television is not a good idea.' So saying, he picked up the remote and turned the TV off. 'What you need to do is close your eyes and relax.'

He scowled when he leant over and saw her eyes were still wide open.

'Scarlet King, do you know you have a problem with obedience? Close your eyes!'

In days gone by—in fact in just hours gone by—Scarlet might have shot back some smart remark. But she was way too preoccupied to indulge in witty repartee at that moment. Way too turned on as well. She could not wait for him to touch her, even if it was just stroking her head. Because she knew that it wouldn't end there.

So she closed her eyes and held her breath, waiting in an agony of anticipation for her seduction to begin.

CHAPTER THIRTEEN

WHEN his fingers first contacted her forehead, Scarlet stiffened inside. When they slid upwards into her hair, her teeth clenched down hard in her jaw. It was a struggle not to cry out. But she managed. Just.

Her mother used to stroke her head when she'd been sick as a child, her touch soft and soothing. John's equally gentle touch might have had the same relaxing effect if she hadn't been so agitated. No, not agitated—excited. Impossible to relax when your nipples were tight and tingling. Soon, it wasn't her head she wanted him to stroke but other more intimate parts of her body. Her breasts. Her belly. Her quivering thighs. Her headache had receded, replaced by waves of dizzying desire which were as demanding and decadent as the bed she was lying in. Scarlet could not believe how much she wanted John to undress her. No longer did she care if he thought her breasts too small. She wanted his hands on them. And his mouth.

If she'd been bold, she might have told him of her cravings. But that was one thing she'd never been in the bedroom—bold.

At the same time, she was driven to say something, anything, which would indicate she wanted him to move on.

'My headache's gone,' she murmured.

John's hand stilled in her hair, but it didn't move on.

Scarlet's eyes opened so that she could work out what he was thinking.

No luck with that, however. She should have known she wouldn't be able to read his thoughts. John had never been one to wear his heart on his sleeve, or his innermost thoughts on his face.

'Maybe I should go back to my room?' she said, battling to hide dismay from showing in her face.

John let out an exasperated-sounding sigh. 'I thought I told you to stop over-thinking everything. You're staying right where you are, Scarlet.'

'I am?'

'Yes. You want this as much as I do. If you didn't, you wouldn't have stayed in the first place. You'd have told me to get lost, then walked off back to your room. If there's one thing I know very well about you, it's your stubborn nature. You never do anything you don't want to do. You *want* me to make love to you, Scarlet, so why don't you just admit it?'

Scarlet glowered up at him, his outburst firing up the urge to tear his egotistical words down in flames with some verbal lightning bolts of her own. But what would be the point? He was right. So very irritatingly right!

But that didn't mean she had to admit to *too* much. He would become insufferable if she confessed to what was really going on in her head, and in her body.

'I suppose there's no point in making you wait any longer,' she said dismissively. 'Not if you're that desperate. It's almost tomorrow, anyway. But don't go imagining I'm panting for it.'

He smiled a very knowing smile. 'We'll see, Scarlet. We'll see...'

Scarlet tried to think of something clever to retort but her brain had shut down the moment his hand withdrew from her hair and dropped down to the top button of her pyjamas. She held her breath whilst he flicked it open with one hand, grateful that his eyes were following his hand and not still looking into her frozen face. Slowly but deliberately he moved on to the next button, then the next, till all five were open, by which time she wasn't panting for it. But she *was* in danger of dying from lack of air in her lungs.

Her sucking in breath sharply brought his eyes back up to her own.

A frown bunched his dark brow together. 'You want me to stop?'

She shook her head.

'Good,' he said. 'Because I don't think I could have.'

His admission of the intensity of his own need soothed Scarlet's worry over the almost uncontrollable nature of her own. It wasn't like her to want a man this much. It was a surprise, but not an entirely unpleasant one. There was something right about enjoying the process of conceiving a baby, rather than what she'd been doing at the clinic. Not that she was likely to fall pregnant tonight. In her experience of charting her cycle each month, it was impossible. Sperm did not live for a week.

'You're thinking again,' John warned her softly. 'Have to stop that, Scarlet. Focus on what I'm doing to you and nothing else.'

He didn't have to tell her twice, especially when he parted her top, exposing her breasts to his eyes.

'So beautiful,' he murmured, cupping her left breast with his free hand and lifting it slightly before bending his head to the nipple.

John didn't suck it the way other men had sucked her nipples, like they were drinking their favourite beer through a straw which was too small. He didn't suck it at all at first. He licked it, slowly, almost lasciviously, wetting it over and over till she moaned in frustration. Even then he didn't suck it. He nibbled at it, then nipped it, then took it carefully between his teeth and tugged it, sending a dagger of dark pleasure stabbing through her entire breast. When he did it again, she twisted to one side, wrenching the burning nipple out of his mouth. She might have voiced some protest had he not pushed her roughly back against the pillow then silenced her with a kiss, which was nothing like the kiss he'd given her earlier. It was hard and hungry, obliterating all thought with a speed which Scarlet would later find astonishing. His mouth didn't abandon hers till she was way beyond anything but lying there, dazed, whilst he undressed her totally and started doing all those things she'd imagined him doing under the covers.

But there were no covers involved. There was nothing to hide her eyes from what was happening to her. She lay there, legs and arms spreadeagled, whilst his hands and lips became stunningly intimate with every inch of her body. And did she care? Not in the least. She moaned with pleasure then groaned with frustration each time he stopped, always when she was just on the verge of coming. It was a mad mixture of near ecstasy followed by sheer agony.

'Oh please,' she begged when his mouth abandoned her swollen clitoris one more tormenting, torturous time.

'Patience, Scarlet,' he said, at which point she swore at him, using a four-letter word which she rarely used. He only smiled and said, 'Soon, sweetheart.'

Her head whirled as he rose from where he'd been lying between her legs and moved up the bed to lie down next to her, propping himself on one elbow.

'Trust me,' he added, giving her a breath-stealing kiss on her parted—and, yes, *panting*—lips, before sitting up and stripping off his black boxer shorts, exposing a stunningly formidable erection. Long and thick, it stood up ram-rod straight. Scarlet couldn't stop staring at it, her mouth drying as she tried to imagine how it would feel inside her.

When he lay back down next to her, she couldn't stop herself reaching out to touch him.

It was the kind of involuntary action John had hoped eventually to evoke in Scarlet, to make her forget about babies and think only of sex. It was what he'd planned when he'd asked her to come up to Darwin a week early. He'd thought he would need a good while to totally seduce Scarlet into such an erotically charged state of mind. It seemed, however, that he might achieve his goal a lot quicker than that. She was definitely not thinking of anything but sex right at this moment.

John knew he should probably stop her doing what she was doing, but he simply could not. Her fingertips felt like butterfly wings fluttering against his engorged flesh. Never before had his penis been touched like that. So sweetly yet so sensuously. It stirred him to an almost unbearable level of arousal. Being with Scarlet was testing his willpower to the limit. He'd already lasted a long time without release...enough was enough.

'No more, Scarlet,' he said, and reached out to still her hand with his. 'I'm only human, you know,' he added with a soft smile when her rather glazed eyes lifted to his.

Scarlet could not believe she'd been so bold as to touch him like that. Or that she'd loved it— loved the feel of him, so hard and yet so soft. It came to her as John lifted her hand away that she might not mind putting her lips where her hand had been—an astonishing thought, given she'd never been keen on that particular form of foreplay. Not that she hadn't tried it once or twice. She had; men seemed crazy about it. But she'd hated the way it made her feel. She'd never imagined for one moment that she might actually enjoy it. Or be turned on by it. But she rather suspected she would be, if she did it to John. Just the thought of doing it turned her on. So did the thought of taking him into her body. A wave of naked desire brought a frustrated groan to her lips.

'What is it?' he asked. 'What's wrong?'

'Just do it to me,' she said, her eyes as pleading as her voice.

He stared down into her flushed face as he positioned himself between her thighs.

'Lift your knees,' he commanded. 'Place the soles of your feet flat on the mattress.'

Her stomach tightened as she did so, her heart pounding against her ribs.

His entry was slow and gentle, but it still brought a gasp to her lips.

He didn't stop, pushing in further till she was filled to the hilt. But he wasn't finished. Another gasp escaped her lips when he suddenly took her by the ankles and wrapped her legs up around his waist. This new position seemed to allow him to slide in even deeper, by which time Scarlet could not wait for him to move.

When he didn't, she did.

Scarlet lifting her hips from the bed evoked something close to panic in John. Never before had a woman been able to make him lose control. Now, suddenly, he was overwhelmed by a powerful urge just to *take* her! Without finesse. Without further waiting or watching. His body began to move quite involuntarily, not slowly or gently, but vigorously, almost violently. Back and forth. Back and forth. She moved with him, squeezing him mercilessly, making his teeth clench down hard in his jaw as he tried to resist the sensations which were threatening to tip him over the edge with humiliating speed. In desperation he grabbed her hips, holding her still with a brutal grip whilst he tried to slow things down— his own body especially. But it would not be denied. There was no hope of lasting much longer, he realised with dismay. No hope at all!

CHAPTER FOURTEEN

SCARLET'S mouth dropped open when she came, so astonished was she by the intensity of her climax. Never before had she experienced spasms so powerful, or so pleasurable. Never before had she made such sounds, moaning and groaning in a wildly wanton fashion as her flesh contracted around his. But any sound she made was soon eclipsed when John came. Holding her even tighter, he shuddered violently into her, his head thrown back, eyes shut.

When his orgasm finished, his head dropping forward, his eyes opened to reveal an expression which Scarlet could only describe as confused. But any confusion was gone as quickly as it came, leaving Scarlet to wonder if she'd imagined it. By then he was smiling—though the smile was sardonic.

'You're not even a teeny tiny bit frigid, Scarlet,' he said in droll tones as he removed her legs from his back and let them flop back onto the bed. 'In truth, you have the makings of a great courtesan.'

Scarlet, who was in the throes of coming back to earth, found herself thrown down with a thud by this last remark.

'Well, thank you very much,' she said tartly. 'What a lovely compliment, saying I'd make a great prostitute. Now, if you don't mind...' She lifted her shoulders and wriggled her hips in a vain attempt to eject him from her body.

A foolish move, for all it did was remind her how it felt with him inside her. Such blissful sensations did not lend themselves to her staying angry.

'I *do* mind,' he said sternly. 'It's very comfy, the way we are. So stop being silly, lie back and just relax.'

It did seem silly to keep struggling.

'Much better,' John said when she slumped back against the pillows. 'Now, how about the relaxing part?' he went on. 'Breathe in deeply and then let the air out slowly. Yes. That's the way.'

Despite doing as he suggested, Scarlet was still not totally relaxed.

'For your information,' John said, cupping her face with his hands before sliding his fingers up into the hair, 'a courtesan was not a common prostitute, but an attractive and often poor

woman who made her living by using her erotic
skills to ensnare herself a wealthy lover. She was
much valued by her patron. He would often buy
her a house, hire staff for her and pay her bills,
all for the privilege of having exclusive access
to her very beautiful body.'

'How interesting,' Scarlet said, finding herself perversely flattered by his words. It was
somehow seductive for a girl to be told that she
could be so brilliant at sex that a man would do
that much to have her. Such praise was as corrupting as words of love.

'What kind of erotic skills did a good courtesan possess?' she asked, her curiosity piqued.

John positioned himself more comfortably
on top of her, his bent forearms pressing into
the bed on either side to ease his weight off her
chest whilst his lower half remained intimately
locked with hers.

'They were many and varied,' he informed
her. 'But a good courtesan concentrated on dis-
covering what her lover liked best in bed, what
foreplay he enjoyed the most, what fantasies he
had. And then she catered to them all.'

'So what fantasies do *you* have?' she asked.

John looked down into her wide blue eyes and
considered how he should answer that.

Not the truth, of course. Most of his sexual
fantasies were too decadent to be voiced aloud.

At the same time, there were some fantasies which could be safely indulged in if and when the opportunity presented itself. John had often fantasised over having Scarlet at his sexual beck and call. It was a temptation impossible to resist.

'That's for me to know and you to find out, my darling Scarlet. Because you're going to become my courtesan for the duration of your stay here.'

'What?'

'You heard me.'

'That wasn't part of our deal.'

'No. It came to me when I discovered how good you were in bed.'

'Oh,' she said, and stared up at him. He really was rather wicked. And very knowing about women.

'Have you done this kind of thing before?' she suddenly asked.

'What kind of thing?'

'Don't play dumb, John. You know what I mean. Is role playing one of your fantasies?'

'No. I just thought it would be fun, that's all. Why, aren't you up for it?' he said in the kind of challenging fashion which he knew she wouldn't be able to resist. Scarlet was nothing if not competitive. Or she had been, at school with him. It had killed her whenever he'd beaten her in an exam.

Scarlet's first reaction was to fire back, *Yes, of course I am.* But hard on the heels of that pride-driven urge came the stark reality of the situation. A courtesan she was not. John was flattering her when he said she was good in bed. She wasn't; not usually. If she'd been good just now, it was because she'd been so incredibly turned on. She didn't even know what she'd done to make him say that. Was it when she'd touched him? Or later, when she'd been writhing around under him? There'd been nothing skilled about that. She'd just gone crazy with need. Just thinking about it was turning her on again.

John sucked in sharply when he felt her move against him.

The little minx! She was answering his challenge by showing him what she could do.

'Obviously your answer is yes,' he said thickly.

'Now *you're* being silly. I don't have the experience or the expertise necessary for such a role.'

'That's a matter of opinion,' he muttered through gritted teeth.

'You can do it to me again, if you want to,' she said, her eyes having gone as smoky as her voice.

He had every intention of doing so, especially when she lifted her legs and wrapped them around him. But the moment he started moving, it happened to him again, that rush of adrenaline which heralded his earlier loss of control. He tried to slow everything down but his body had a mind of its own, and he surged deep into her with almost manic determination. Immediately, he was in danger of coming. *Immediately.* In desperation, he withdrew and flipped her over, pulling her up onto her knees under him, giving himself a few precious seconds of relief before he plunged into her again. Her instant cry of release came to the rescue of his battered pride, allowing him to stop his futile struggle. Eventually, they collapsed together onto the bed, John pulling her sideways into a spoon position so that he didn't squash her with his weight. When he wrapped his arms tightly around her and held her close she sighed a happy-sounding sigh. Soon, her breathing slowed and she slipped into that wonderfully sound sleep which often came after great sex.

Unfortunately, John wasn't so lucky, sleep eluding him as he tried to work out why he'd rocketed so out of control, not once but twice.

The only logical reason he could find was that Scarlet was *nothing* like his usual woman. Despite her age, she was a relative innocent where sex was concerned. Innocent and touchingly sweet, which could also be a factor in his uncharacteristic responses to her.

John's choice of bed partners these days were

not of the innocent and sweet variety. After he'd left university—where no-strings sex was a common pastime—John had quickly found that sleeping with his female peers in the wider world was hazardous to his peace of mind. Most girls around his age didn't want one-night stands; they expected him to stay for breakfast. Expected him to ask them out again. Expected to become his steady girlfriend. In short, they wanted commitment, something John wasn't interested in. He enjoyed the bachelor lifestyle. Enjoyed being free to come and go as he pleased without having to answer to anyone, or upset anyone.

John soon realised that if he wanted to have a reasonably regular and guilt-free sex life he'd have to choose older women to sleep with, ones who weren't looking for love and marriage. Recently divorced was good, he'd found, along with the occasional career girl who was already married to her job. During the past couple of years, he'd favoured women whose only interest in him was an evening of pleasant company, usually over dinner, followed by a long night of sexual pleasure—always at their place. That way he didn't have to ask them to leave in the morning. He could do the leaving, when and if he chose.

Bianca had once asked him why he didn't bring his 'girlfriends' home. He'd told his housekeeper that *she* was the only real girlfriend he had, which had made her laugh.

His heart twisted as he always did when he thought of Bianca.

Best not think about her then, buddy. You can't change what happened.

Scarlet stirred slightly in her sleep, pulling up her knees and thrusting her very shapely bottom against his stomach, causing his till-then deflated sex to come to life once more with alarming speed.

It was impossible to sleep here now, common sense dictated, John smothering a groan as he very carefully withdrew from her oh-so-delicious body, scowling when he saw the evidence of his renewed desire for her. Truly, this was getting ridiculous!

He threw Scarlet a rueful glance as he quietly rose from the bed and dragged on his boxer shorts. *Frigid?* She was about as frigid as Darwin in the summer.

CHAPTER FIFTEEN

SCARLET woke to solitude and silence. She blinked several times, then sat up, pushing her hair back behind her ears as she cocked her head and listened for the sounds of life.

Nothing.

She had no idea what time it was, a quick glance around showing no clock anywhere. The light coming into the room from the balcony suggested it was late. Quite late, a suspicion confirmed by the urgency of her need to go to the bathroom. Scarlet was grateful for John's absence as she threw back the covers and jumped, naked, from the bed. Though that didn't stop her wondering where he was. He'd certainly been in bed with her when she'd fallen asleep.

Oh Lord!

Scarlet could not believe how incredible the night had been. How incredible *he* had felt. Maybe size did matter.

But of course it wasn't just John's size which

had made last night different from any other night she'd ever spent in bed with a man. She'd been beside herself with the most dizzying pleasure long before he'd stripped off. What John didn't know about a woman's body clearly wasn't worth knowing. He was an extraordinary lover—imaginative and very patient during foreplay, but passionate and primitive when it came to the act itself. She hadn't forgotten the sounds he'd made when he'd come the first time; how they'd reminded her of a wild beast.

Had that been a subconscious fantasy of her own? she wondered as she washed her hands then stared up at herself in the vanity mirror. To be taken by a wild beast?

She would never have imagined so. But who knew what lurked in the dark recesses of one's mind?

There was one fantasy that in the cool light of day she decided definitely didn't appeal to her—that of being a courtesan. Especially John's courtesan. No way would she enjoy kow-towing to his every sexual whim and wish, Scarlet told herself firmly as she finger-combed her messy hair into place.

On the other hand, she did not regret—or resent—the degree to which she'd enjoyed his love-making. It was exciting, in a way, to discover that with the right lover she was actually highly sexed.

No doubt John was somewhat smug over his successful seduction of her, but *c'est la vie*. It would be hypocritical of her to start pretending this morning that she hadn't enjoyed every single moment. Saying so to his face, however, might prove difficult. She still hadn't overcome her shyness, not to mention her pride.

Her pride was one of the reasons she was reluctant to leave the bathroom before checking that the bedroom was still empty and the bedroom door firmly shut. As much as she hadn't worried about John seeing her naked last night when she'd been turned on, it was a different matter in the cold light of day. Hurrying back into the bedroom, Scarlet scooped up her pyjama top from where it was lying on the rug beside the bed, donning it quickly before going on a frantic search for the bottom half. She found the shorts under the covers, right down the bottom of the bed. Once they were safely on, she made the bed then, after taking a few calming breaths, went in search of the man himself.

She almost missed him, sprawled sound asleep on one of the sofas, only the sound of his deep but even breathing attracting her attention. Scarlet shook her head as she stared down at his half-naked form, amazed that he could sleep like that without a rug or a blanket for warmth. Okay, so the apartment was air-conditioned, but still…

He really did have a great body, she thought for the umpteenth time as her admiring eyes began travelling over him from head to toe, stopping abruptly when they reached the scar on his right leg, just to the side of his knee. She hadn't noticed it last night, but then she'd been somewhat distracted at the time. It was quite a nasty scar, purple and puckered around the edges, probably the result of that accident he'd had recently when he'd broken his leg. She wondered how the accident had happened and how bad it had been. If he'd been a normal man, she could have asked him about it. But John wasn't a normal man, she conceded ruefully. He had this thing about being questioned. Silly, really, but so darned typical of him. He'd always been a loner, with a loner's persona. 'Tell 'em nothing and take 'em nowhere': that was obviously his creed in life where women were concerned. It surprised Scarlet that he'd ever admitted to having this long-held desire for her. To do so must have gone against the grain.

She was still puzzling over this conundrum when she spotted an empty glass lying on the rug next to the sofa, right where John might put his foot when he finally woke up and stood up. Scarlet went round, picked the glass up and took a sniff. She didn't much care for brandy but she knew the smell well, having used brandy often when making Christmas cakes. The fact that John had left the bed and sat out here, drinking, till he fell asleep was another puzzle. Why hadn't he stayed with her?

Scarlet was standing there, trying to find an answer when she realised John was stirring.

For a split second, she contemplated bolting for the bedroom but, as she'd told him last night, when she was nervous about something, she liked to get it over and done with as soon as possible.

She waited and watched whilst John stretched and yawned first before one lid flickered upwards, then another.

'Good morning, Scarlet,' he said as he swung his long legs over the side of the sofa and sat up. 'I presume you slept well?'

'Very,' she admitted, determined to be honest. Determined to make him answer some questions as well. 'Why did you come out here to sleep?'

'For that reason,' he replied somewhat drily. 'To sleep. I was, shall we say, struggling to concentrate.'

'Oh,' she said, and blushed.

'No need to be embarrassed. It's not your fault that you're a beautiful woman. I knew, if I stayed there, I wouldn't be able to keep my hands off you. So I came out here and left you to have a good night's rest.'

'That was…very considerate of you,' she said, not sure now if she felt embarrassed or pleased. There was something incredibly seductive about a man admitting he couldn't keep his hands off you.

'My pleasure, Scarlet. But don't worry,' he added with a wicked little smile. 'You can make it up to me today.'

She gripped the glass tightly whilst trying to imagine what he had in mind. 'What time is it, do you know?'

'Time you and I had some breakfast, after which you can join me in the shower.'

'But…'

'No buts, Scarlet. We had a deal, remember?'

Scarlet straightened her shoulders. 'I don't re-call agreeing to sex morning, noon and night.'

'No?'

'No.'

'Are you saying you don't want to join me in the shower?'

'I'm saying you are not to presume that I will agree to anything and everything. You are to ask me first. And respect my wishes. Otherwise, this deal is off and I'll catch the first flight home.'

'Have you forgotten why you came up here in the first place?' he reminded her ruthlessly.

'I haven't forgotten,' she said with a defiant tilt of her chin. 'But that doesn't change my stance. Take it or leave it.'

Damn it but she was calling his bluff! Not that it had been a bluff, exactly. He'd thought after last night she'd be putty in his hands this morning. He supposed he should have known better. This was Scarlet he was dealing with here.

'Very well,' he conceded. 'I would love you to join me in the shower after breakfast, Scarlet. But if you don't want to, that's fine,' he added through clenched teeth.

Scarlet wasn't sure what to say now, the ease of his capitulation having surprised her. She actually wanted to join him in the shower. It was his arrogant manner which had got her back up. Now that he was asking politely, it seemed rather hypocritical to say no. But she felt she had to. To give in at this early stage would feel somehow like she'd lost the battle—as though she—or, rather, her body, she hastily corrected—belonged to him. After last night, she wanted to make sure she stayed in control, and that meant setting boundaries.

'I'd rather shower by myself,' she said, trying not to sound too prim and proper. 'I'm not used to sharing showers. Or making love during the day time, for that matter. If you don't mind, could we confine our sexual activity to the evenings?'

'I'd be lying if I said I didn't mind. But you're calling the shots for now, so sex will be confined to the evenings. Until you change your mind, of course,' he added with a wicked glitter in his bedroom-blue eyes. 'That is a woman's privilege, isn't it—to change her mind?' And so saying, he stood up and stretched once more, grimacing as he did so. 'Thank God I won't have to sleep out here tonight. It's hell on my back.'

'You could have slept in one of the guest rooms,' she pointed out somewhat tartly.

'Now, why didn't I think of that? Right, do you want breakfast before your shower or after? Note, I'm asking very politely and not telling you.'

Scarlet pulled a face at him. 'There's no need to be *that* polite. I also don't expect you to wait on me hand and foot. You showed me where everything in the kitchen was last night. I can easily get myself some cereal and juice, which is all I usually have for breakfast.'

'Splendid. I'll leave you to it, then. I'm off to have *my* shower. A very long, very cold one.'

Regret consumed Scarlet as she watched him stalk off. But she refused to back down. She needed to keep focused on what she'd come here to do. As John had inadvertently reminded her, this wasn't a pleasure trip, no matter how much pleasure she might have felt last night. And, actually, Scarlet remembered reading that too much sex was as bad for conception as too little. Couples who were having trouble falling pregnant were encouraged to chart the woman's cycle and reserve sex for the days surrounding ovulation. She would have to mention that to John. But not yet, perhaps. She suspected he would not take kindly to her telling him he would have to curtail his pleasure for a couple of days early next week so that his sperm count would be at maximum level.

But tell him, she would. Eventually.

No matter what, she had to maintain some control over John. *And* herself.

Pursing her lips determinedly, Scarlet marched out to the kitchen where she swiftly set about getting herself a bowl of muesli and a glass of orange juice, all the while making plans for the day in her head. As soon as she had breakfast, she would shower and dress—in the main bathroom—after which she would ask John to take her for a walk around the CBD of Darwin, followed by a light lunch somewhere, followed by a long drive or a boat trip on the harbour, or whatever would fill in the afternoon.

She would make sure it was late afternoon by the time they came back to the apartment, leaving only enough time for them to both freshen up before going out for dinner, which should occupy a further few hours. Although usually a fast eater, she would be very slow this evening, making sure that it would be at least ten or eleven by the time they got back to the apartment, with their energy levels low after a long day of walking and sightseeing. She doubted John would be capable of making love to her more than once. Twice, at best. He did seem to have amazing stamina in that regard. But what the heck? She was sure she would survive two more ground-shaking orgasms without totally losing her willpower or, worse still, imagining that she must be in love with John simply because she was enjoying sex with him.

Her top lip curled derisively as she dismissed that insane possibility without a second thought. Only hopelessly naive romantics believed in such hogwash, and it had been some time since Scarlet had been either naive or a romantic. She supposed in one way it was rather sad to have one's illusions about love and sex dashed to the ground so emphatically. But then real life was sad, wasn't it? Real life killed off one's father when you were only nine. And real life kept you unloved and childless till you were at such an age that your dreams were almost beyond your reach.

But only almost...

Scarlet wasn't sure why, but she suddenly felt supremely confident that when she caught her flight home on Sunday week she would be pregnant with John's child. Okay, so having a baby was only half of her dreams, but it was the better half. The safer and more secure half. She would settle for that half, any day of the week.

Her heart thudded in her chest as she tried to imagine how it would feel when her pregnancy was confirmed. She would be over the moon. And so would her mother.

'Oh my God, Mum!' she exclaimed, having forgotten all about the promise she had made to her mother the previous evening to send her some photos of the apartment today.

So much to do, she thought as she started to shovel the muesli into her mouth. And so little time!

CHAPTER SIXTEEN

SCARLET ate breakfast, had a shower and got dressed in record time, choosing white capri pants and a salmon-pink top which had a not-too-low sweetheart neckline and capped sleeves. The same speed was applied to her hair, which she only half blow-dried before scooping it all up into a high pony-tail, anchored by a white elastic band. Make-up was none, other than some tinted sunscreen plus her favourite coral lipstick. She didn't spray on any perfume or don any jewellery, having resolved not to dress or act provocatively. After adding flat white sandals, she extracted her phone from her bag and set about taking photos of the main bathroom and the floral quilted guest bedroom, careful not to make either look too large or too luxurious.

Once satisfied with her snaps, Scarlet made her way out to the kitchen, half-expecting John to be in there, having breakfast. But he wasn't. She frowned. Surely he'd be showered, shaved and dressed by now? Clearly not, however, the living room proving as deserted as the kitchen. His bedroom door remained shut, she noted, so it was likely he was still in there, but no way was she going to knock, or go in search of him. Instead, she returned to the kitchen, where she took a couple of photos of just one section before moving back to the living room and shooting only a fraction of that area, getting in just one of the sofas and rugs.

It wasn't till she went out onto the balcony with the intention of snapping the spectacular harbour view that she found John sitting out there with some toast and coffee. No doubt he'd showered but he hadn't shaved, looking like a beach bum with the stubble growing on his chin and nothing on but a pair of bright board-shorts.

A very sexy beach bum.

'So here you are!' she exclaimed, doing her best not to stare at his beautifully bare chest, resentment rising with the thought that *he* was being deliberately provocative. After all, it wasn't that warm out there on the balcony. It was, in fact, quite fresh, with a stiff sea breeze blowing.

'Aren't you cold?' she asked somewhat tartly.

'I never feel the cold,' he said, his eyes lifting to run over what she was wearing. 'We inveterate campers are a tough breed. Taking photos for your mum, are you?'

'I promised her last night.'

'Yes, I heard you. You and your mum are obviously very close. Is that why you're still living with her?'

'I didn't plan to but then I also didn't plan to deliberately become a single parent,' she shot back. 'Once I made that decision, it made sense to stay on at home.'

'But you're *not* going to become a single parent. Not now. You'll have me to help out.'

'Come now, John, even if things work out and I do fall pregnant with your child, I'll still need my mother's support. You're not going to be around most of the time—it isn't part of our deal. You'll be off working in some far-flung corner of the world most of the time and only come home to visit at Christmas every year. More importantly, I *like* living with my mother. We're best friends.'

'I see. Fair enough. Get on with your photos then,' he bit out, and fell broodingly silent.

Scarlet held her tongue with difficulty whilst she took a lot of snaps. Normally, she would have made admiring comments about the beauty of the view. But she didn't trust herself to speak right at that moment. Why she let John get under her skin so much, Scarlet wasn't sure. But he

did. He always had. She had a feeling John felt
exactly the same about her. It was a shame, really, given the situation. If only they could become genuine friends, it would make life so
much easier.

It's up to you then, Scarlet, the voice of common sense advised her. *Don't expect John to
make the move to cease hostilities between you.
Men don't do things like that. It's the woman
who usually makes the peace when a relationship becomes rocky.*

Not that they had a *relationship*. Up till now,
all they had together was a shared childhood
and one night of sex. Great sex, admittedly, but
still just sex. Shared parenthood, however, would
definitely change all that.

The enormity of what they were planning to
do suddenly struck Scarlet like a physical blow,
doubts shooting to the surface of her mind as
she tried to work through what having John as
the father of her baby really meant. It could become quite complicated, she realised agitatedly.
And messy. Going to that clinic and having an
anonymous sperm donor had been a simple plan.
Lonely, maybe, but simple. No one else was directly involved. With artificial insemination, she
was master of her own destiny and the controller
of her child's upbringing. Could she trust John
not to want more involvement once his son or

daughter became a reality? A few of her girl-friends had told her how their husbands had not been so keen when they had become pregnant early in their marriages, but each had become besotted once the child had arrived. Would John have an epiphany once he became a father? It was possible, she supposed.

Scarlet stopped taking endless photographs and whirled to face him.

'I think I might have made a big mistake by accepting your offer,' she blurted out, still shaken by her thoughts.

An emotion close to panic sent John leaping to his feet. 'What?'

'You heard me.'

'I heard you, but I don't understand what's behind such a sudden turnaround. *You* contacted *me*, Scarlet, not the other way around.'

Now she looked decidedly shame-faced.

'I know. I guess I was desperate at the time.'

Desperate. John could not believe how much it hurt, hearing her say that. But then he remembered the way she'd been with him last night. That hadn't been desperation. That had been desire, pure and simple. Not so pure, either. His flesh stirred at the memory of her touching him, of her begging him to just do it to her.

He gritted his teeth as he willed his body to behave itself. This wasn't the right time to use sex to sway her mind. At the same time, if Scarlet thought for one moment he was going to let her leave, then she was dead wrong.

'Why do you think you made a big mistake accepting my offer?' he asked with forced calm as he came forward and cupped his hands over her shoulders.

She immediately clasped her phone with her two hands and held it up against her breasts, as though she was afraid of his chest touching hers.

Good, he thought.

'I just don't think it's wise for you to be the father of my baby, that's all,' she said with her usual stubbornness. 'It could become complicated.'

'In what way?'

'You might change your mind about your level of involvement. You might… Oh, I don't know what you might do, exactly. I just want my son or daughter to have a secure, happy life. I would hate there to be any conflict.'

'Well there certainly won't be any conflict if you don't have a child at all! Which could be the case if you cut and run now.'

'The clinic said I just had to be patient.'

'The clinic has vested financial interests in saying that.'

'That's a horribly cynical thing to say!'

'I'm a horrible cynic.'

'You just don't understand,' she said with a ragged sob.

The sounded affected him. He didn't want to make her cry. He just wanted to soothe her worries and make her stay with him. The thought of her leaving still filled him with alarm.

'But I do understand,' he told her gently. 'I do. You're afraid of my interfering in your role as a parent even though I promised not to. You've lost your trust in men, which includes me.'

'But how can I trust you when I don't really know you any more?'

'Ah. Back to that again.'

'I think it's only fair that you answer at least some of my questions if you're going to be the father of my baby.'

That *was* fair, John accepted grudgingly.

'Okay,' he said. 'Fire away.'

Her eyes narrowed. 'You'll tell the truth?'

'Cross my heart and hope to die,' he said. 'But only if you promise to stop this nonsense about leaving.'

Scarlet thought about that for a second, deciding that she wasn't going to let John steamroll her into anything. It had been foolish of her to come up here without thinking everything through. Uncharacteristically foolish. But of course she *had* been desperate at the time.

'I reserve the right to still leave if I find out

you're not suitable father material,' she told him firmly.

'I thought you found that out last night,' he returned with a wicked little smile.

She blushed. Again.

Scarlet itched to stamp her foot in fury at herself. Blushing was hardly the way to convince John she had the upper hand.

'Must you remind me of that?' she threw at him.

'No need to be embarrassed. Now, how about you send those photos to your mum whilst I go put some clothes on? Then we'll get out of here.'

'But you were going to answer some questions.'

'You can walk and talk at the same time, can't you? Women are always claiming they can multi-task.'

Scarlet wanted to hit him. But not as much as she wanted to kiss him. Oh Lord, she was one mixed-up girl at the moment!

'Must you tease me all the time?' she snapped.

He smiled. 'Absolutely. I find you very sexy when you're angry.'

'Well it's no wonder you've wanted to screw me silly all your life, then,' she retorted, blue eyes flashing. 'Because I've been bloody angry at you since the first day we met!'

He tried not to laugh, but he couldn't help it.

Neither could she. Her lips just twitched at first, then her chin started to quiver. And then they were both laughing, loud and hard.

Their laughter broke some of the sexual tension which had been steadily growing in Scarlet since she'd stepped out onto the balcony and spotted John sitting there with no shirt on. But even as she laughed she knew it would be wise to get out of this apartment as soon as possible. The physical chemistry between them was dangerously strong and extremely seductive, which was perverse, since they didn't see eye to eye about much. She was a person who valued family and community above all else. He was a loner who spurned involvement with others, even his family. She worked to live. He lived to work. Or he used to; she wasn't sure what his work ethics were now that he was rich.

These last thoughts reminded Scarlet of all the questions she wanted to ask John. Questions which had always plagued her about him. She was relieved that he'd agreed to satisfy her curiosity, because what if he hadn't? Scarlet doubted she would really have had the courage to leave. She was too close to achieving her goal of a baby. On top of that the prospect of more sex with John was a wickedly corrupting temptation, especially when she was alone in his half-naked presence. She needed to get him dressed, pronto, then get them both out of here.

CHAPTER SEVENTEEN

JOHN made his way quickly back into the master bedroom where he threw on a white T-shirt, slipped on some ancient but comfy flip-flops, then reached for a white baseball cap which he'd bought last week. He'd discovered that even in winter the sun up here in Darwin could burn, especially now that he didn't have a thick covering of scalp and facial hair to protect him.

When he returned to the living room, Scarlet was waiting for him with a roomy straw carry-all slung over her shoulder and a large-brimmed white sun-hat on her head.

John walked ahead of her to the door, opening it and waving her through before turning and locking up. Slipping the keys into his shorts pocket, he accompanied her along to the bank of lifts where they rode in companionable silence down to the lobby. Once there, he took her elbow and steered her out onto the pavement then safely across the road to the park opposite.

'The park runs the full length of the Esplanade,' he told her as they started walking along the main pathway which wound its way through the extensive lawns and gardens. 'This path will lead us to the far end of the CBD, past Government House, which is a splendid old building, then over a walkway and down a lift to the newly developed waterfront. I think you'll be impressed with what they've done to what used to be a pretty dingy area.'

'You're right—the views of the harbour from down here are incredible! And different from up on your balcony. Do you think we could go out on the harbour one day?' she asked whilst taking photos.

'Of course. I'll charter a boat. We'll go sightseeing and I'll show you how to fish. Fishing's a recent hobby of mine.'

She stopped taking photos and looked at him. 'I'm surprised. I thought you were a *terra firma* man.'

'I thought I was too. But after my accident I couldn't do too much for a few months. A friend suggested fishing and I found I loved it.'

'My dad used to like fishing. But I never went with him. I always thought it would be boring.'

'Not if you know where to fish and you have the right equipment. Then it's quite exciting. And very satisfying. They'll cook us what we catch on board the boat. If you like eating sea-food, that is.'

'Love it.'

'That's one thing we have in common, then.'

Scarlet laughed. 'The only thing, I'll warrant.'

'No. Not the only thing,' he said, his voice low and knowing.

Scarlet deliberately ignored his sexual over-tone by walking over to read a commemorative plaque which had a list of names on it connected with the Second World War. Darwin had been the only city in Australia ever to be bombed during any of the world wars, she'd discovered during the Internet search about the city. Scarlet took a photo of the plaque, then a few more of the view.

'What a lovely place Darwin is,' she said.

'I like it,' he said.

'So why don't you live here permanently, John? Why go back to South America? Come to think of it, why did you choose to work there in the first place? I mean, there are jobs for ge-ologists here in Australia. You could have just come up here, or gone to one of the many min-ing towns in Western Australia. There's no need to go to the other side of the world just to get away from...' The question she really wanted to ask burst out. 'Why *do* you hate your father so much, John?'

'Wow,' he said. 'That's quite a lot of questions in one hit. Look, why don't we sit down over here?' he said, directing her to a park bench that was under the shade of a tree. 'It could take me a while to answer them all.'

'Especially truthfully,' she reminded him.

'Scarlet, would I lie to you?'

'In a heartbeat,' she replied, and he smiled.

'You know me too well.'

'I know you don't like talking about yourself.'

John shrugged. 'I doubt you'll find any of this happy listening, but what the hell? You wanted the truth.'

For a split second, he wondered if he could get away with lying to Scarlet. But only for a split second.

He wasn't about to sugar-coat anything, either.

'First things first,' he said rather bluntly. 'I'm actually not going to go back to Brazil. I recently sold my house in Rio. I plan to stay and work here in Australia.'

'That's a surprise! What made you decide to return home after all these years? I got the impression you loved living in South America.'

'I did. I probably would have stayed living there indefinitely if my housekeeper—a truly sweet lady named Bianca whom I was very fond of—hadn't been killed. Stabbed to death by a gang of street kids she'd been trying to help.'

'Oh, John, that's awful!'

'It was. She was such a good woman. She used to go out every night and take food to the homeless. If I wasn't away working or out clubbing for the night, I'd go with her—not because I was a saint like she was, but because I was worried about her safety. The places she used to go were downright dangerous. I tried to stop her going out alone when I wasn't there, but she took no notice of me. She said she'd be fine. Said if she didn't help those poor kids, who would?

"When I came home early one morning to find a police car parked outside my house, I knew something bad had happened to Bianca. I have to confess I went crazy when I found out she was dead. I wanted to kill the little bastards who did it to her. As it was, I beat the hell out of a couple of them. The police weren't impressed, and gave me a warning. At the time, I didn't give a damn. They weren't doing anything that I could see to solve Bianca's murder. Anyway, I knew if I stayed there, I might do something really stupid so I sold up and left.'

'Just as well you did. Does your family know any of this?'

'Of course not!'

'But why ever not?'

'Because it's my private and personal business, not theirs.'

'So they don't know about your housekeeper being killed? Or that you've left South America for good? Or that you're going to live and work here in Australia in future?'

'Not yet. Wait a second,' he went on quickly when he saw her mouth opening. 'Let me finish before you get on your high horse and start tearing strips off me for being a secretive and unloving son. I will tell them. Well…not the bit about Bianca. Just that I've come home to Australia to live and work. Meanwhile, they're none the wiser and no one is getting hurt.'

Scarlet pressed her lips tightly together to stop herself from telling him that he was always hurting his family by his long absences, especially his mother. Carolyn had been quite upset when he'd left so soon after her party. She'd be even more upset if she knew he was up here in Darwin, holidaying, whilst she thought he was in Brazil working.

'Now, if you must know the truth, I do not actually *hate* my father. My emotions where he is concerned are not that simple.'

Scarlet blinked. What on earth could have possibly happened to sour the relationship between father and son so?

'You won't know this since my parents don't speak of it, but I was born a twin.'

'A twin!' Scarlet exclaimed, totally taken aback.

'Yes. I had a brother, Josh, born a few minutes before me. We were identical twins. Identical in genes but, as is often the case, not identical in nature. He was the extrovert; I, the introvert. He was hyperactive and rather naughty, but a real little charmer. He could talk when he was just a toddler. I was quieter and much less communicative. People thought I was shy but I wasn't. I was just…self-contained.'

Scarlet had an awful feeling about what was coming. After all, no twin brother named Josh had moved into the house opposite hers. She braced herself for bad news but it still shocked her.

'Josh drowned in our back-yard pool when he was four,' John went on. 'Mum was on the phone one day and we were playing outside. Josh pulled a chair over to the child-proof fence and attempted to climb over it. But he fell off the top of the fence and hit his head before toppling into the pool. I stood there for far too long in shock before running screaming for my mother. By the time she pulled Josh out of the pool, he was dead.'

'Oh, John,' Scarlet choked out as tears welled up into her eyes. 'How tragic.'

John stiffened when he saw the evidence of her sympathy. This was what he could not stand. This was why he'd never told anyone this story. Because he didn't want to feel what he was feeling at that moment—as though he was somehow to blame for Josh's death. Logic told him it couldn't possibly have been his fault, but logic meant nothing to a four-year-old seeing his mother almost catatonic with shock and his father weeping in despair. It welled up in him again, the guilt and the grief. Because he'd loved Josh just as much as his parents. He'd been his twin brother. His flesh and blood. They'd been inseparable from birth.

But no one had cared about *his* grief.

John could not believe how painful he still found the memory. Damn it, he would not show weakness in front of Scarlet.

'To cut a long story short,' he said abruptly, 'My father did something the night after Josh's death which affected me very badly. When I saw him sitting in an armchair in our lounge, with his head in his hands, I ran up to him and put my arms around him. He pushed me away and told my mother to put me to bed, that he couldn't stand to look at me.'

Scarlet sucked in sharply. What a dreadful thing for John's father to say!

'Later that night, he did come into my room to kiss me goodnight, but I turned my face away and refused to let him kiss me. He just shrugged and walked away. After that, I stopped speaking

to him altogether for a very long time. In fact
I totally ignored him for years. He didn't seem
to mind or care. He was no longer the father I'd
once adored. He was just an empty shell of a
man. My mother could see what was going on
but she was a mess herself for ages and didn't
seem to know what to say or do to make things
right. She didn't recover till she had Melissa. She
was the one who insisted we sell our old house
and move—for a fresh start, she'd said. It made
no difference to Dad. Or to me. He became a
grouch and a workaholic and I became what you
know I became. An angry, resentful boy.'

Scarlet had started gnawing at her bottom lip
to stop herself from weeping. What a sad, sad
story. Her heart went out to John as she began
to understand what had made him the way he
was. How incredibly hurt he must have been. No
wonder he retreated into himself. And no wonder he didn't stay around his family for too long.

'I'm surprised you're as civil to your father as
you are,' she said with feeling.

'He's mellowed since he retired. I can't say
that I've totally forgiven or forgotten, but hatred
and revenge never get you anywhere. Now that
I've grown up, I can see that parents aren't perfect. They're just human beings. Josh had been
the apple of Dad's eye and Josh was dead. Grief
can make you say dreadful things.'

He had said appalling things to Bianca's family after she was killed, blaming them for not going with her that night. They'd been amazingly understanding of his grief and had not taken his accusations to heart. But he'd still felt terrible afterwards, once he calmed down. It was one of the reasons he'd given them his house and everything in it. To make it up to them.

'Have you ever confronted your Dad over what he said and did that night?' Scarlet asked, frowning thoughtfully.

'No.'

'At least your mother loved you and your brother equally,' she pointed out.

'I'm sure she did. But then Melissa came along, and Mum simply doted on her.'

'All mothers dote on their daughters, John. It didn't mean she loved you any less. To be fair to your mum, by then you were not the most lovable boy in the world.'

John laughed. 'Trust you to make me stop pitying myself.'

'That wasn't my intention. But do you know what, John? Things might not have been quite the way they seemed back then. I've been thinking...'

John sighed a weary sigh. 'What about this time?'

'About what your father said that night. He

might have meant he couldn't stand to look at you because you reminded him of Josh. You were physically identical, after all. It might not have meant that he didn't love you just as much as your brother.'

'Pardon me, but I think his subsequent actions rather confirm that he didn't. He had every opportunity over the years to be a loving, caring father to me but he wasn't. He acted like I didn't exist. You've no idea how jealous I used to be of *your* father. Now he was what a father should be.'

'He was rather wonderful,' Scarlet agreed. 'But at least you had a great grandfather.'

'True. Grandpa was very good to me. To be honest, if it wasn't for him, I probably would have run away from home and ended up in jail.'

'Oh, surely not?' Scarlet protested.

'Why not? Jails are full of angry young men, Scarlet. Neglected sons with little self-esteem and no goals in life. My grandfather gave me back my self-esteem, plus the goal of becoming a geologist. I was shattered when he died just before my graduation. But even in death, he looked after my well-being by willing me some money. Quite a lot of money, actually. With it came a letter, telling me to travel and to see the world. So as soon as I graduated, I took off. First I went to Europe, but strangely Europe didn't appeal to me all that much. Too many cities and not enough trees maybe! I took off again and travelled all around for about two years.

"Eventually I reached South America. By that time, I had run out of money so I had to find work or go home. As you can imagine, going home didn't appeal all that much. Anyway, because I had no actual work experience, the only job I could get was with a speculative mining company who were looking for geologists to go places most people weren't prepared to go. It was dangerous work, but the money was good, and I found I rather enjoyed taking risks. Over the last decade, I discovered a new emerald mine in Columbia, oil in Argentina and natural gas in Ecuador.

"In return, I got shot at several times, fell off a mountain, almost drowned in the Amazon and was bitten by more vicious insects than you could ever count. Still, for my blood, sweat and tears I got paid serious bucks. I was able to buy myself that house in Rio and this apartment here in Darwin. I now don't have to take jobs which might get me killed!' He smiled wryly. 'I can even afford to support a child and give his or her mother enough financial freedom that she doesn't have to work for the rest of her life. If she doesn't want to,' he added.

Scarlet hadn't even given John supporting

her financially a second thought. Now that he'd brought the subject up, she realised it was a tricky situation. If she accepted his money, it would give John more rights. Custody rights, maybe.

Her forehead scrunched into a frown as she once again considered the consequences and complications which would come with John being the father of her child.

'More thinking, I see,' John said before she could voice an answer to her concerns. 'And not happy thoughts either. Look, if you don't want my money, then just say so. I won't ram it down your throat. Most women would be happy to have that offer on the table, but I should have known you're not most women.'

'I do value my independence,' she admitted.

'With my money you could buy yourself your own place. You could even employ a nanny, if you want to stay working.'

'A nanny? I don't want to hand my baby over to a nanny! As for buying my own place, I'll have you know I already have enough money to buy my own place, if I wanted to. I've been saving for a house ever since I started work. Thank you very much for your offer, John, but no; I don't want or need your financial support.'

Her stance shouldn't have annoyed him. But it did.

'Fine,' he bit out. 'I won't pay for a damned thing.'

'There's no reason to get angry,' Scarlet countered sharply. 'You should be glad that I'm not most women. Just think what would happen if I were a gold-digger. I could take you for heaps!'

In spite of himself, John's mouth quirked. She looked so disgusted by the very idea. Her anger had flushed her cheeks and made her look even more beautiful than usual. 'Fine. I accept that it's a good thing you aren't a gold-digger. Now, are there any more questions I have to answer before we can proceed with my plan for today?'

Scarlet blinked her surprise. 'You have an actual plan for today?' She'd thought *she* was the one with the plan.

'I did have. Before you put a spanner in the works and started wanting to get to know me better.'

'Well I… I…' Scarlet could not believe she was stammering when she was usually so articulate. She pressed her lips tightly together and took a deep breath before continuing.

'Okay. Fine. No more questions for now. But I might have some more later,' she added as an afterthought. *When I can think more clearly, that is.* 'So what was your plan for today?'

'A brief hour of sightseeing followed by a light lunch, followed by an afternoon in bed.'

Scarlet's mouth was suddenly bone dry. 'The whole afternoon?'

'That's a compromise. When you first walked out onto my balcony this morning looking good enough to eat, I wanted to whisk you right back into bed and keep you there all day.'

She just stared at him, the extent of his desire for her still a shock. So was the extent of her desire for him. Suddenly, her earlier resolve to restrict sex to the evenings dissolved, as she herself was dissolving.

'Also,' he went on with a sudden flare of desire in his eyes, 'this afternoon has nothing to do with babies and everything to do with pleasure. Not just mine, either. Judging on how you reacted last night, your sex life so far has been sadly lacking. I aim to rectify that, if you'll let me.'

Let him! How in earth was she going to stop him?

John rose to his feet and held out his hand to her. 'Now. Let's go sightseeing.'

CHAPTER EIGHTEEN

SCARLET was impressed by the waterfront development. It was tourist heaven, with luxury apartment blocks, a fantastic hotel, chic shops and cafés, great walkways suitable for morning jogs, a wave pool to delight children and adults alike and deep-water wharves at which cruise ships could dock. Scarlet might have made lots more complimentary comments if she hadn't been rendered uncharacteristically quiet by what was going on in her head, and in her body.

Never before had Scarlet felt such agitation. Her head whirled. Her stomach swirled. When John suggested they have some lunch at a trendy outdoor café, she was swift to agree, because it meant she could finally take her hand out of his. Not that she didn't enjoy holding hands with him. She did, more than she wanted to. But it wasn't the kind of physical closeness she was craving.

It had been wickedly clever of him to tell her

what he had planned for this afternoon, she realised as they sat down opposite each other.
Clever and corrupting. For she could think of
nothing else now. She couldn't even make up
her mind what to eat, telling him to order for
her. John didn't seem to be similarly afflicted,
ordering their lunches with the kind of *savoir
faire* she should have expected from this new
John. He didn't even consult the menu as he
told the pretty young waitress to bring them two
chicken-and-salad wraps on Turkish bread and
two mugs of latte.

The girl's simpering smile showed she found
John just as attractive as Scarlet did.

She almost made some caustic remark after
the waitress hurried off to do his bidding, biting her tongue just in time. But the near-miss
left Scarlet somewhat rattled. If she didn't know
better, she'd think she was jealous. Which was
insane! There was absolutely no reason to be
jealous because some slip of a girl was dancing
attention on John. After all, she wasn't going
to be spending the afternoon in bed with him.
Scarlet was!

She sucked in sharply at the spite-filled pos-
sessiveness behind her thoughts.

'Something wrong with what I ordered?' John
asked straight away.

'No, no. It was fine. I just remembered I should

have taken some photos whilst we were walking around to send to Mum,' she improvised. 'I totally forgot.'

And no damned wonder, she thought mutinously. *All I've been thinking about is having sex with you all afternoon, you wicked man!*

'You can still take some photos after we've had our lunch.'

'Yes, I suppose so.'

'But you'll have to be quick.'

'Oh? Why's that?' she asked, glancing up to the sky to see if there were any clouds gathering. But no, the sky was still clear and blue.

Some clouds had gathered in John's eyes, however, by the time her gaze returned to his.

'For an intelligent thirty-something, you can be pretty dense sometimes.' There was total exasperation and another kind of tension in his voice. 'I'm getting the sense that you don't know much about men, Scarlet.'

Scarlet decided not to take offence. She was tired of arguing with John. 'I'm well aware that I've led a narrow kind of life. After listening to all your travelling tales and adventures this morning, I would say *very* narrow. I dare say you probably think I've had a lot of boyfriends over the years but in truth I can count the number on one hand. So, no, I don't know all that much about men. I'm sorry if that disappoints you.'

John didn't want her apology. He wanted her naked in his arms. It had been hell this last hour, showing her the sights and resisting the temptation to drag her back up to his apartment posthaste. As for his being disappointed that she'd had only a handful of lovers, nothing could be further from the truth. It pleased him hugely. He loved that he could show her things in bed that she didn't know. Her lack of experience excited him. So, strangely, did her lack of feminine guile. Maybe he'd spent too many years bedding women who could read a man's needs like an open book, and who knew how to meet those needs every which way. Whatever the reason, he'd never felt such a need for any other woman.

But he would clearly have to wait a little longer. He could hardly insist that Scarlet skip the lunch he'd just ordered. Or forget taking those damned photographs for her mother. As much as John sometimes regretted the tenuous relationship he had with his family, he did not miss the demands that some parents made on their children, even into adulthood. Being a grown up, in his opinion, was being able to do your own thing without having to answer to someone all the time. Clearly, Scarlet was aghast at the lack of communication which existed between himself and his family, but he could think of nothing worse than having to ring his mother every single night he was away. Sometimes, months went by without his contacting home. He rarely felt guilty about it. Scarlet would, however. Underneath that tough exterior she liked to show to him, she had a soft, sentimental and sensitive soul.

This last realisation warned him not to say or do anything to hurt her. Now *that* would make him feel really guilty.

'Nothing about you disappoints me, Scarlet,' he said truthfully. 'I have always admired you enormously.'

'Really.' There was a trace of laughter in her voice.

'Really.'

'Even when I'm being dense about men?'

'Even then.'

'So what was I being dense about a minute ago?' she asked.

'I thought you would intuitively know that I needed to get you back to my apartment after lunch, as soon as possible.'

John saw the penny drop in her eyes, and colour flare up in her cheeks.

'Oh,' she said, then smiled a rueful smile. 'I thought it was just me suffering in silence.'

Her admission did little to soothe John's own frustration. He could not recall ever being this hard.

It was a relief that their lunch arrived at that

precise moment, giving his overheated brain some well-needed respite. His overheated body as well. The wrap was excellent, though he hardly noticed, considering the speed with which he ate it.

'You'll get indigestion,' Scarlet warned him with a sweet smile. She was taking her time, he noted.

'Just eat your food and get on with those photos or I'll take them for you,' he ground out.

'Yes, sir!'

'And stop being sarcastic; I prefer the way you were a little while ago.'

'Which was?'

'Soft and sweet.'

'But I thought you said that my being stroppy turned you on?'

John spoke through gritted teeth. 'I don't want to be turned on any more right at this moment.'

'Ah, I see. Not to worry. I promise to be sweet as apple pie till we're safely behind closed doors.'

John had to laugh. 'Just get on with your food, will you?'

'I don't think I can eat any more,' she said.

Their eyes met across the table.

'Get those photos taken while I'll go pay the bill,' he said thickly as he rose to his feet.

Scarlet took only a few photos before he returned to collect her.

They hurried back the way they'd come, not holding hands this time, and not talking at all. Scarlet struggled to keep up with his long strides, her breathing heavy by the time they reached his apartment building. They rode the lift up in silence, Scarlet not daring even to look at John for fear of what he might do right there in the lift.

By the time John opened his apartment door and ushered her inside, she was desperate for him. Up against the door would have done. Or on the sofa. Or even on the floor. She imagined John would have been just as eager, so she was surprised when he didn't pounce immediately. Surprised and disappointed, especially when he stepped right away from her.

'No, Scarlet,' he said brusquely when she frowned at him. 'Not here and not yet. Now, I want you to go into the main bathroom, strip off and have a long, hot shower. I'll be doing the same in my bathroom. When you feel nicely relaxed, get out of the shower, dry yourself off then come into my bedroom. Without any clothes on, please. No towel. No robe.'

Scarlet swallowed. 'You...you expect me to walk into your room totally naked?'

'Totally. You have an incredibly beautiful body, Scarlet, and I want to see all of it, all the time.'

'All the time?' she choked out.

'Absolutely. Clothes are only going to be worn in future when we go out.'

'But...'

'No buts. This is part of my plan.'

'What plan is that?'

'A private plan.'

'But I don't see how—'

'I thought we agreed no buts,' he broke in sharply. 'And no more arguments. All I want to hear from you this afternoon is "yes, John; of course, John; anything you say, John".'

'You forgot "three bags full, John",' she snapped, but he could see the excitement in her eyes.

He smiled. 'That's my girl.'

Scarlet shook her head at him. 'You are the most infuriating man!'

'And you are the most desirable woman. Now, go and do exactly as you were told.'

He didn't wait for her reply, stalking off into the nearby master bedroom and shutting the door behind him, leaving her standing in the middle of the living room feeling totally flummoxed. But oh, so turned on. There was no question that she wouldn't do as he'd commanded. Because, deep down, she *wanted* to do it.

Doing it, however, was quite daunting. She didn't look at herself in the bathroom mirror after she stripped off, keeping her eyes averted as she turned on the shower and waited till the water was warm enough to step into. She washed herself all over, doing her best not to linger too long on those areas which reminded her of how excited she was. Five minutes later she was out of the shower and reaching for one of the thick turquoise towels.

It took Scarlet another five minutes before she dared leave the bathroom, during which time she brushed out her hair for ages before freshening up her lipstick and spraying on some perfume. When she could not delay her emergence any longer, she scooped in several deep breaths then opened the bathroom door.

Walking naked through the apartment was the hardest thing she'd ever done, harder than showing up at that fertility clinic the first time. Which had been darned hard. By the time she reached the door to the master bedroom, Scarlet was a bundle of nerves. Steeling herself, she decided not to knock, choosing instead to open the door and go straight in.

As she entered the room, John was just coming out of his bathroom, a white towel wrapped low around his hips.

She ground to an annoyed halt, her hands in her hips. 'I want you naked too,' she threw at him.

'Not just yet,' he replied. His eyes glittered

as they flicked over her from head to toe. 'You are even more beautiful standing up than lying down. Now, come over here to me. I want to watch you walk, then I want to hold you hard against me and kiss you till you beg me to just do it to you like you did last night. But not in bed— standing up with your legs wrapped around my waist and your arms tight around my neck.'

The highly erotic images his words evoked made Scarlet's head spin. How she managed to cross the room without tripping or stumbling she had no idea. But cross it she did, despite her knees feeling like jelly. He watched her closely with narrowed eyes, not saying another word. When she drew near, she could hear his heavy breathing and her own. Could feel his tension and her own. When he tossed the towel aside, she could see his arousal.

Stunningly, magnificently erect. A lethal weapon of naked desire. Her mouth dried in anticipation of his doing it to her the way he'd said he would, standing up. Her heart rate quickened, her nipples tightening.

Oh yes, she thought heatedly when he reached out to pull her into his arms, pressing her hard against him so that his erection sank deep into the soft swell of her stomach. *Yes, yes. Do it to me. Do it to me now. Don't kiss me. Don't wait. Just lift me up and do it!*

He didn't obey her silent commands. He kissed her first, hot hungry kisses which brought her to a level of frustration she could not previously have imagined. It was violent, the need to have him inside her. The need to come. When a muffled moan echoed in her throat, John tore his mouth from hers.

'Tell me that you want me, Scarlet,' he whispered fiercely into her hair.

'Yes, yes, I want you,' she choked out. 'Oh God, John, just do it. Do it the way you said.'

She gasped when he drove up into her, then again when he cupped her buttocks and lifted her right off the floor.

'Wrap your arms and legs around me,' he ground out.

After she did so, he carried her over to the bedroom wall, using it to support her back whilst he surged up into her, over and over. Her release was quick and savage, her first spasm so intense that she screamed out. He came too, just as violently, his orgasmic groans sounding more like cries of pain. His fingertips dug into her flesh whilst she clasped him just as tightly around his neck. Their climaxes lasted a considerable time, their bodies pulsing together, their hearts thudding to the same mad beat.

Finally, it was over, a wave of post-coital exhaustion bringing a heavy sigh to Scarlet's lips.

John sighed also, his head lifting from where he'd buried it in her hair.

Scarlet felt absolutely drained. In fact, she was having difficulty keeping her legs where they were. They were on the verge of dropping back down to the floor when John carried her over to the bed, tipping her gently back across the black quilt before slowly withdrawing.

'See what you've done to me?' he said as he straightened and nodded downwards.

'Poor John,' she murmured sleepily. 'Perhaps you should lie down next to me and have a rest.'

'Perhaps I should. But only on condition you don't ask me any more questions.'

CHAPTER NINETEEN

'HAVE you had a lot of women?' Scarlet asked.

She was lying across the bed with her head resting on John's stomach, her face turned towards his, her left hand playing with the mat of damp curls on his chest. John was stretched out with his hands linked behind his head and his eyes on the ceiling. They'd not long returned to the bed after a rather lengthy shower.

'You promised not to ask me any more questions.'

'I did no such thing. I just let you off while you were resting. So I repeat...have you had a lot of women?'

'Yes,' he replied bluntly. 'I've had a lot of women.'

'I thought as much.'

'Does it matter?'

'I suppose not.'

'Not jealous, are you?'

'Not at all. Just curious. But when did you

have time to have all these girlfriends? From what you told me, you've spent most of your adult life climbing up mountains and trekking through jungles.'

'I didn't say I've had lots of girlfriends, Scarlet. I said I've had lots of women. There's a difference.'

'Oh. Oh, I see. You're a one-night-stand type of guy.'

'Generally speaking, yes. I had a couple of steady girlfriends at uni but nothing serious. I don't have time for long relationships these days. Or the inclination.'

'But I'm sure you told me the night of your mum and dad's party that you'd just broken up with some woman.'

'I lied.'

She sat up abruptly. 'But why?'

'To avoid you asking me questions, of course.'

Of course...

As much as Scarlet wanted to know everything there was to know about John, she knew when she was beaten. He'd already told her more than she thought he ever would. To press further could spoil things. He was already glowering at her.

'Okay,' she said. 'No more questions.'

'Thank goodness. Silence is golden, you know, especially when one is totally knackered.'

Scarlet laughed, then lay back down with her head on his stomach. This time, however, she was facing the other way. She glanced down at his penis, which wasn't totally knackered. But wasn't erect, either. It didn't look quite as daunting when it was like that. She suspected, however, that she only had to take it into her mouth and it would soon be revived.

'Hey!' he exclaimed, when she took hold of his penis with a firm grip. 'What in hell do you think you're doing?'

'What do you think I'm doing?'

He groaned when she began sliding her hand up and down, her fingers tight around his flesh.

'Woman, you have no pity in you.'

'Not for you, I don't.'

'You're going to be the death of me.'

'Possibly. But what a way to go.'

He laughed, then gasped. 'Don't you dare do that!'

She didn't answer. She couldn't.

John's jaw clenched down hard at the sensations which were rocketing through his body. Damn, but she was good at that. Hard to believe her claim that she had so little sexual experience. Yet he did believe her. Scarlet was no liar. *He* was, however, when need be. His protest over her going down on him had been a lie of sorts. He'd wanted her to do just that. Wanted her to re-arouse him. Wanted her to have climax after climax.

Because that was his plan, to make her body addicted to having sex with him. And then, next Monday, two days before she entered the period when she was most likely to conceive, the sex would stop, giving his sperm count time to recover and her body time to become increasingly needy. By Wednesday, she'd be ready to fall pregnant, her mind not on babies so much but on pleasure.

It was a perfect plan, John thought as he reached down and splayed both his hands into her hair, meaning to stop her. After all, he didn't want to get her addicted to *giving* pleasure, but in receiving it. But, damn it all, it was delicious, what she was doing. His fingertips pressed hard into her scalp. Instead of pulling her off him, he found himself holding her head captive whilst he spun out of control and surrendered to temptation.

Afterwards, when she crawled up the bed to snuggle against him, he wrapped an arm around her shoulder and pulled her close.

'That was incredible,' he said, trying not to sound as shaken as he still felt. 'Thank you.'

'My pleasure,' she murmured, and pressed her still-moist lips against the base of his throat.

His heart squeezed tight as a wave of emotion washed through his body.

I'm the one who's getting addicted here, he realised. *Addicted and involved. Emotionally involved.*

The idea that he might be falling in love with Scarlet was so surprising, so startling, that John didn't know what to think or do. It seemed an impossible idea at first. He didn't do love. But gradually, once he put aside his initial shock, John began to see that it wasn't such a weird idea. He even considered the possibility that he'd been a little in love with Scarlet ever since his teenage years.

'You're going to think me very naive,' she said suddenly, lifting her head up enough to lock eyes with him. 'But I used to think that I would have to be madly in love with a man before I really enjoyed sex. I mean *really* enjoyed it, the way I have with you.' Her head lowered again to rest across his chest. 'I guess that comes from being a hopeless romantic all these years. I didn't re-alise that all it would take was a man who knew what he was doing in bed.'

The ironic timing of Scarlet's statement did not escape John. But her very sensible words were a relief in a way. Of course it wasn't love he felt for Scarlet. It was still lust, the same thing he'd always felt for her. Too much great sex with her was addling his brain. He needed to stop for a while.

'Thank you for the compliment, Scarlet,' he said. 'I've also made a discovery about myself and sex since going to bed with you.'

Her head lifted again. 'What's that?'

'I can't keep going for ever.'

'Neither can I. In fact, I can't even keep my eyes open,' Scarlet said as she snuggled back down, her head on his chest, her right arm flopping across his rib cage.

'I could do with a sleep too,' John said, glad she couldn't see the grimace on his face. How in God's name was he going to go to sleep with her lying all over him like that?

He didn't, of course. He just lay there beneath her, struggling to control his breathing, and his body. Scarlet fell asleep first, for which John was grateful, because it enabled him to move her off him onto the bed. She immediately curled up into the foetal position, John covering her naked body with a sheet before rolling right away from her.

Once he'd put some physical distance between them, John began to relax. But it was still quite a while before he surrendered his mind and body to the welcoming oblivion of sleep.

CHAPTER TWENTY

SCARLET was taken aback when she woke and saw that the sun was so low in the sky. She must have been asleep for a couple of hours at least!

It wasn't like her to sleep during the day. Of course, it wasn't like her to have so much sex during the day. Or any sex at all. She'd read somewhere that having a climax was the best sleeping pill in the world. No wonder she'd passed out. In fact, it was a wonder she'd woken up!

John was still out like a light, she noted as she rolled over.

All due to moi, Scarlet thought rather smugly.

'Poor darling,' she murmured, stroking his arm gently till he stirred. When he rolled onto his back and opened his eyes she sat up and smiled down at him.

'Time to get up, sleepyhead. I don't know about you but I'm starving. Is there a local restaurant you know which opens early?' she asked as she swept her hair back from her face. 'I don't think I could wait too long before I eat something.'

The sight of her bare breasts was doing wicked things to John's nicely rested body. But he checked the impulse to seduce her right then and there, reminding himself that the quicker and earlier they ate dinner, the longer the evening would be.

'The sailing club serves dinner from five-thirty,' he informed her. 'It's only a few minutes' drive from here, dress is casual, the seating *al fresco* and the sunset's worth taking your camera for.'

'Sounds perfect. Meet you in the living room in fifteen minutes,' she said. Jumping out of bed, she dashed for the door, no doubt heading for the main bathroom and guest bedroom where she'd left all her things.

'Scarlet!' he called out before she could make her escape. She turned in the doorway, no longer shy about showing him her body, he noted. That was a good sign.

'What?' she asked.

'A dress please. And no underwear.'

She blinked, then flushed.

'No buts,' he ground out. 'No arguments. No underwear.'

Her chin came up, her eyes defiant. 'No,' she threw back at him. 'I'm not going to do that.'

'Why not? You'll like it.'

'No, I won't.'

'How do you know you won't?'

'I just know.'

'Like you know you won't like camping? Or fishing? Yet you haven't tried either. Give it a go, Scarlet. No one will know but me.'

'That's one person too many. I agreed to have sex with you, John. I didn't agree to anything... kinky.'

His eyebrows arched. 'I would hardly call that kinky.'

'I would.'

'Fine. I wouldn't want you to do anything you weren't comfortable with.'

'I don't intend to. Now, I'm going to go get dressed.'

It was a rather irritated John who rose and set about getting dressed himself, pulling on fresh underwear, a pair of jeans and a black T-shirt. Obviously he had a way to go before Scarlet's mind was totally consumed by sex. *He* was the one who was plagued with that problem. His agitation was not improved when Scarlet made her appearance right on schedule, wearing a very pretty floral sundress with a flouncy skirt, tight waistline and a halter-necked bodice. Her blonde hair was bundled up rather haphazardly on top of her head, with lots of wispy strands kissing her face. She didn't appear to be wearing make-up other than some lip gloss. Even so, her cheeks glowed and her blue eyes sparkled. She looked fresh and beautiful and so sexy, it was criminal.

'You're not wearing a bra,' he said gruffly, spotting the outline of provocatively naked nipples.

She shrugged, the action bringing even more attention to her unfettered breasts. 'Some dresses aren't made for bras.'

'Whatever,' he said offhandedly, doing his best to get some perspective in the face of his escalating frustration. But it wasn't easy. He hadn't realised that his plan to seduce Scarlet into a state of permanent arousal would back-fire on him so painfully. He wished now that he was wearing shorts and not hip hugging, hard-on-squashing jeans. But he could hardly change clothes at this late stage.

'I suggest you bring a jacket or a cardigan,' he advised her sharply as he headed for his front door. 'It might get cool after the sun goes down.'

'I'll go get one.'

He made no comment, not wanting to delay their departure any longer. The sooner he got her out to the sailing club, the sooner they could eat and the sooner they would be back here, at which point she would do as she was told for once!

Scarlet didn't say a word during the ride down in the lift, or the drive to the sailing club. In truth she was feeling guilty. And very uncomfortable. Because she had actually done what John had so arrogantly demanded she do, gone out without any underwear on.

Of course, no way was she about to admit it. She'd just wanted to have the experience. Wanted to see if he was right.

He wasn't, she realised very quickly. She didn't like it. The braless bit didn't overly bother her. It wasn't the first time she'd gone braless, though she didn't make a habit of it. Having her bottom bare under her dress, however, made her feel terribly vulnerable. Fearful, even. What if a wind blew her skirt up and people saw that she had no panties on?

Every muscle she owned tightened just thinking about such a horrifying and humiliating event.

By the time they arrived at the sailing club she was extremely tense. Thankfully, there was no breeze blowing. The air was still and quite warm so she didn't need her shawl, and didn't have to worry too much about any unfortunate wind accidents.

It was a smallish establishment, Scarlet saw

straight away, built on a select plot of land right
on the harbour. Despite its prime location, there
was no pretension about the single-storey club-
house, or the outdoor eating areas. The tables
and chairs were a mixture of wooden and plas-
tic, several of them set up right at the water's
edge under the shade of tall palm trees. Because
they were early, they were able to get one of the
best tables where no one would be able to block
out the view of the sunset. The sun was by then
extremely low in the sky and beginning to turn
a gorgeous golden colour. Its beauty distracted
Scarlet temporarily from any concerns over her
panti-less state.

'How long before it sets?' she asked John as
she sat down.

'Not long. Time to start taking some photos.
I'll go order the food. What would you like? You
can have steak and salad, fish and chips, a roast
or Chinese.'

'Fish and chips sounds good.'

'Fish and chips it is, then.'

Scarlet got her phone out and started clicking away whilst he was gone, amazed at how
the gold colour intensified as the sun sank even
lower in the sky. By the time John returned, it
was just touching the horizon, its colour now
closer to red than gold.

'Thank you,' she said when he placed a glass

of chilled white wine on the table in front of her.
'But I can't drink it just yet. I don't want to miss
a moment of this.' And she turned her attention
back to the sunset.

It amazed her, just how quickly the sun set.
One minute the edge of the circle was just touching the horizon, the next the sun was halfway
gone then, poof, totally gone.

'Oh…' she said with a regretful sigh.

'Darwin is famous for its sunsets,' John said.

'They're pretty spectacular. Mum is going to
want to come up here after seeing these photos.
Which reminds me,' she said as she put down
her phone and picked up her glass of wine. 'I
have to ring her later. Don't let me forget.'

'Are you going to ring your mother every single night?' he asked somewhat impatiently.

Scarlet took a deep swallow of wine and
counted to ten before answering. She understood
that John's relationship with his family was way
different from hers. But that didn't give him the
right to be critical of what she believed was a
normal way to act.

'Yes, John,' she said at last, firmly but calmly.
'I'm going to ring my mother every single night.
I love Mum very much and I know she'll be
missing me. I'm sorry if you find that annoying
but that's just too bad.'

She waited for him to say something sarcastic

back, but he didn't. He just nodded. 'I've always admired your spirit, Scarlet. And your honesty.'

Scarlet's hand tightened around the stem of the wine glass. 'I'm not always honest.'

John slanted her a surprised look. 'Really? Do tell.'

Talking about her mother had made Scarlet think about all the lies she'd told her before coming here. And all the lies she'd have to keep telling her every single night of her stay in Darwin. After all, she could hardly tell her the truth. Still, this train of thought did pose the question of what she would eventually tell her mother if and when she did fall pregnant to John. How would she explain it?

It shocked her that she hadn't worked out a plan concerning this problem earlier. Shocked her, too, that she'd almost forgotten about why she'd come up to Darwin in the first place. Her mind had been focused on nothing but sex for most of today. She'd gone to sleep this afternoon thinking about sex. Had woken thinking about sex. And had left off her underwear, thinking about sex.

It was worrying, this craving John had created in her to experience everything with him. Every sexual position. Every form of foreplay. Every erotic game. And, yes, even the kinky ones.

Suddenly, sitting there with no underwear on

was no longer slightly embarrassing. It was seriously shameful yet at the same time so wickedly exciting that she could actually feel the heat between her thighs.

'Scarlet?' John prompted. 'What haven't you been honest about?'

'I…um… I was thinking about the lies I've told Mum. It's going to be awkward, explaining things later.'

'You mean when you fall pregnant.'

'*If* I fall pregnant,' she corrected.

'When. If. Whatever. It's a little early to start inventing stories yet. We'll worry about that when you're actually pregnant.'

'I'm sorry to be a worry-wart, John, but I need to have some story settled in my mind tonight. It's really bothering me.'

'Okay,' he said, trying to be patient. 'The way I see it, you have two possible stories to choose from. You can tell your mum the truth, or you can say you ran into me by accident whilst you were on holiday up here and we had a brief fling.'

Scarlet shook her head. 'That last idea won't fly. Mum won't believe it. Neither will your parents. Even if they did, they'd wonder what you were doing in Darwin when you were supposed to be in Brazil.'

'Then tell them the truth.'

'Which is?'

'That you told me you desperately wanted a baby the day of their party, and out of friendship I offered myself as the father, no strings attached. You can say we planned to meet in Darwin that night but kept our assignation a secret from everyone in case you didn't fall pregnant.'

Scarlet frowned. 'I suppose that seems reasonably plausible. Mum would believe it, since she knows about my failed artificial-insemination plan, but I'm not sure about your parents. After all, we've always come across as enemies, not friends.'

'Rubbish. Mum never thought that and Dad doesn't think at all. We'll go with the truth, if and when the time comes. Okay?'

'I suppose so.'

'Look, Scarlet,' he said firmly. 'I brought you up here early so that you could relax and have some fun. Forget about the future for the next few days and just think about enjoying yourself.'

'That's what I've been doing.'

'What's wrong with that?'

'I'm not sure what we've been doing is fun, exactly.'

'Then what is it?'

'Dangerous.'

'In what way dangerous?'

'I might get to like it too much.' *And to like* you *too much*, came the sudden thought.

'Sex, you mean?'

'Yes.'

'I can't see how that's dangerous.'

'You're not a woman.' Women had a long history of falling for men who were great lovers. Scarlet didn't want to fall for John. That would not be a good idea at all.

The buzzer rang at that moment, announcing that their meals were ready. John shook his head at her as he picked up the buzzer and stood up.

The food was excellent, the fish cooked in beer batter and the chips crisp and hot. The smell of the food reminded Scarlet how hungry she was and she set about eating the meal with gusto. The time it took to eat the meal was a blessing as well, for it gave her the opportunity to calm down. Of course she wasn't falling in love with John! She was just being silly and naive. Still, if she was going to keep on having sex with him— and she definitely was—then she had to adopt a more casual attitude to sex and get a grip on her emotions. Okay, so sex with him was earth-moving stuff—wasn't she a lucky girl?

Such thoughts did little to dampen her escalating desires, however. By the time they left the club for the short drive home, Scarlet was near to bursting with frustration. She suspected that

John was of a similar frame of mind. His eyes kept returning to her cleavage. Which meant he was sure to pounce the moment they were alone. That would have suited Scarlet fine, except for the little matter of being butt-naked under her dress. Her pride simply would not let John discover that she'd done what he wanted after all.

'I'm going to ring my mother first,' she said the second John closed the apartment door behind them.

'Fine,' he growled. 'I've got a couple of calls I have to make, anyway.' And he marched off in the direction of the kitchen.

Scarlet scuttled off to the guest bedroom where she quickly pulled a pair of white satin panties out from her case and put them on. Once that was done, she sat down on the side of the bed with her phone in hand and punched in her home number. It rang and rang, but her mother didn't answer. When the phone clicked over to the answering machine, Scarlet thought about leaving a message but decided not to. She didn't want her mother to call her later when she was otherwise engaged. Instead, she rang off then tried her mother's mobile number, even though she knew it was probably turned off. Her mother was of that generation who only used their mobile phones for making emergency calls. She never thought to leave it turned on so that people could call her.

But, surprisingly, it was on, her mother answering after only a few rings.

'Mum!' Scarlet said with surprise in her voice. 'You actually turned your mobile on.'

'I thought I should. I knew you'd ring me tonight and I didn't want to miss your call.'

'Where on earth are you? It sounds rather noisy.'

'I'm at Erina Fair, doing some food shopping. What you can hear is the rain on the roof. It hasn't stopped bucketing down since you left.'

'No rain up here. It was about twenty-five degrees today, with just a gentle breeze blowing off the sea.'

'You're having a good time, by the sound of you.'

Good…

Now that wasn't a word which sprang to mind about today, Scarlet thought guiltily.

'I haven't been doing all that much,' she said. 'Went for a long walk around the city and down to the new waterfront area which was pretty amazing. I'm just back from dinner at the sailing club.'

'The sailing club, no less! That sounds swish.'

'Actually, no, it's nothing like that at all. The club's on the small side and very casual. Where you eat is right on the water and has a great view of the sunset. I took lots of photos. Which reminds me, have you looked at the photos of the apartment I sent you?'

'I sure did. It looks lovely and the view is fantastic.'

'I've taken heaps more photos today. I'll email them to you as soon as I get off the phone.'

'Oh, don't worry about doing that, love. I'd much rather you showed me the rest of your photos when you get home. That way you can tell me all about them at the same time. So what are you going to do tomorrow?'

'I'm not sure. I haven't booked anything as yet. I might just potter around Darwin again, or sit on the balcony and read a book.'

Or I might spend all day in bed, fulfilling every single sexual fantasy I've ever had.

'You do whatever you want to do, darling. And don't worry about calling me every day. You're up there to have a complete break. And it's not like I'm lonely. I'm with the girls at the salon all day, then I'm going to my quilting meeting tomorrow night. And Carolyn has kindly asked me over to her place for dinner on Saturday. I dare say she thinks I'm missing you, and of course I am. But not in a sad way. I love it that you're having a holiday. I tell you what—

leave off calling me till Sunday night. By then you'll have lots of news to tell me.'

'Okay. I'll ring you on Sunday night around seven. Bye, Mum. Look after yourself.'

'You too, darling. Love you. Bye.'

Scarlet sighed as she hung up. Her mother *was* missing her but trying desperately not to show it. Perhaps it was a good thing for her mother to learn to cope by herself for a while.

It was just as well, however, that she didn't know what her daughter was up to during her 'holiday'. She would be seriously shocked.

Scarlet could no longer pretend to be shocked. The lust which was consuming her was also obliterating both shock and shame. She could not wait to be with John again. Her heart beat quickened as she hurriedly made her way back out into the kitchen where the object of her desires was just saying goodbye to whoever he was talking to.

He placed his phone down on the kitchen counter and looked over at her.

'I expected you to talk for a lot longer than that.'

'The line wasn't good,' Scarlet informed him, amazed at how calm she sounded. 'It was raining so hard I could hardly hear her. Who were *you* talking to?' she asked, still managing to keep up her cool facade. Underneath, however, she was all liquid heat.

'That was a mate of mine. Owns a helicopter. His name's Jim. Before that I rang another mate, Brad. He owns a boat-charter business. I've been lining up our activities for the next three days. Tomorrow, we're going on that harbour cruise, the one where you learn to fish. Saturday, we're going to visit Kakadu and a few other tourist spots by air, then late in the afternoon Jim is going to set us down in a very special place where I'm going to show you that camping can be fun too. Sunday morning, Jim'll come back to collect us, then we're going to do a spot of heli-fishing before coming back here and cooking our catch. How does that sound?'

'Wonderful.' In truth, she didn't give a damn what they did tomorrow. Or Saturday. Or Sunday. All she could think about was here and now.

'John?' she said, her voice turning throaty as desire trickled like shards of hot ice down her spine, radiating out into her breasts and her belly and every other turned-on area of her body.

'Yes?'

'Could you please stop talking now?' she choked out. 'I really need you to make love to me.'

John stared at her, his gaze so hungry and hot Scarlet thought she would combust on the spot.

'In that case, I really need you to take that dress off,' he said in a low, gravelly voice. 'If you recall, I did say that no clothes were allowed when we were alone together.'

Scarlet gulped. Thank God she'd put her panties back on. As wickedly charged as she felt, she still didn't want John to know that she'd sat through dinner without any underwear on. Now that *would* be shaming. Her heart missed several beats as she reached up her back to find the zipper which anchored her dress in place. Seconds later the dress was on the floor and her pulse rate went off the Richter scale.

'Now the rest of it,' he ordered.

Her hands trembled as she took her panties off, but not through nerves. It was sheer excitement that was making her shake. Tossing the panties away, she straightened her shoulders and stood before him, totally nude, except for her shoes.

'Scarlet King,' he said as his heavy lidded gaze raked over her. 'You are one wickedly beautiful woman.'

I'm one very wicked woman, Scarlet thought, her belly tightening when he began to walk around the benchtop towards her.

Even before he pulled her into his arms, she knew that she would do anything John asked of her tonight. Anything at all.

CHAPTER TWENTY-ONE

Late Sunday afternoon

'I STILL can't believe how much I like fishing,' Scarlet said as they walked back to the apartment, John carrying a bag of provisions they'd bought at a nearby supermarket. 'I quite liked it on Friday but I really enjoyed myself this morning.'

They'd not long returned from their helifishing expedition, which had involved being delivered by helicopter to a special river spot where the barramundi had practically jumped onto their lines. They'd caught too many, really. They'd given Jim a few and still had five to bring home, stashing four in John's freezer and keeping out a large one which Scarlet planned to cook for them both tonight, hence the trip to the supermarket.

'I quite liked the camping part as well,' she added, though perhaps it was the place she'd loved more than roughing it in the outback. The spot John had chosen to camp next to last night had been extremely beautiful, a fresh-water billabong surrounded on three sides by rugged cliffs, and fed by a waterfall which had sparkled like diamonds in the late-afternoon sun.

He slanted her a smug smile. 'What you liked, madam, was sharing my sleeping bag.'

Well, yes, she certainly had. It had been something else, sleeping like spoons in the one sleeping bag with their arms around each other and their bodies joined, John making love to her on and off during the night. But it wasn't the amount of sex which Scarlet began thinking about now, but the quality of John's love-making. It had been different to what he'd done to her on previous nights. His love-making in the sleeping bag had been slow and gentle, and rather wonderful. It had left her feeling not ravaged, so much as loved. They'd talked at length too, exchanging memories of their childhood, laughing about incidents which had once bothered them both.

Dared she hope that their relationship was deepening? That John might care for her as she was certainly beginning to care for him?

It was impossible to pretend it was just lust she still felt for the man. She liked John's company, in bed and out. Liked his friends. Liked his surprisingly warm, easy-going way.

'I have to say I was surprised how well you took to going feral,' he said with amusement in his voice.

His comment surprised her. 'What do you mean, feral?'

He grinned. 'Once I convinced you that no one could possibly see you, you loved skinny dipping in the billabong. And sitting by the campfire naked.'

'Don't be crude,' she said sharply.

'And don't you start being a hypocrite,' he shot back. 'There was nothing crude about anything we did out there. It was fun.'

Fun? *Fun?* Was that what being with her still meant to him? Just *fun?*

It was a dismaying reality, but logical. John didn't fall in love. Even if he was capable of it, he simply didn't want to.

Unfortunately, the opposite was true of herself—she *did* want to. Also unfortunately, she had an awful feeling that she already had. She'd foreseen this disastrous outcome the night they'd gone to the sailing club. What a fool she was to think she could stop it happening!

Dear God, how could she possibly have John as the father of her child now? At the same time, how could she not?

She was damned if she did, and damned if she didn't.

Her eyes searched his for a hint that maybe she was wrong. Maybe his feelings *had* deepened for her. But all she saw in his face was irritation and impatience. If he cared for her—even a little—he would understand that what they'd shared last night had been something special, not just *fun*!

'You're not going to start a fight, are you, Scarlet?' he asked her somewhat warily. Her heart sank. She wasn't. Of course she wasn't. But it wasn't going to be the same after this, was it? She was sure to keep hoping for more from John. Hoping and praying. And it would never happen. Yet if she had his baby he'd be in her life for ever. And she'd be secretly in love with him for ever.

'I think we should get back to the apartment,' she said stiffly and, whirling, set out purposefully along the pavement.

John shook his head as he trudged after her. Everything had been going according to his plan. Absolutely everything. She'd clearly become addicted to sex with him. Extremely addicted. And he'd been only too happy to oblige. Frankly, he'd never before felt the buzz he felt when he was with her. She could fire him up with just a look. He couldn't get enough of her. She was so damned hot, and so damned obliging.

Up till now, that was...

'What's wrong?' he asked her during their ride up in the lift.

Scarlet was still struggling with the enormity of her realisation, so she didn't have a ready or a reasonable answer for him.

'Nothing's wrong,' she bit out.

'Don't take me for a fool, Scarlet. My using the word fun upset you. I'm not sure why.'

'Yes, well, I obviously don't have as casual an attitude to sex as you do. I'm not a one-night-stand kind of girl. What we've been doing to-gether...it's all been a bit much. To be honest, it's beginning to bother me.'

'Right. I see.'

The lift doors opened and they made their way along to his door. John extracted his keys from his shorts pocket, all the while thinking that Scarlet had just handed him the perfect ex-cuse to put a halt to the sex till she was entering the phase when she'd be likely to conceive late on Tuesday night. Not that he wanted to stop the sex. Hell, no. He'd been looking forward to making love to her after dinner as he had every other night, a shudder of dark pleasure running through him as he recalled how total her sexual surrender was. She never said no to him any more, no matter what he wanted to do. It was going to be hard, giving that up for two days.

Under the circumstances, however, it would be wise if she spent tonight in the guest bedroom. His only problem was how to suggest it. That might be awkward. As much as Scarlet claimed she didn't like having sex for sex's sake, the truth was that she did. A lot.

John was thinking about how he could solve this problem whilst he opened the door. He didn't say a word as he walked in and headed for the kitchen with the shopping, leaving Scarlet to close the door and trail after him. The ring tone of a phone—not his—suddenly split the silence in the apartment. Scarlet ran off into the guest bedroom where she'd obviously left her mobile. John heard her answer but then she closed the door, shutting him out.

Ten minutes later, she emerged. John knew immediately that this time, something was really wrong.

'That was Joanna,' Scarlet said before he asked. 'She's one of the hairdressers at the salon. Mum had a fall on Thursday when she came home from shopping. Slipped on some wet tiles and broke her wrist. Her right wrist. The thing is, John, I have to go home.'

'Hold on a minute,' John said, his stomach instantly churning. 'What do you mean, you *have* to go home? Why do you *have* to go home? I'm sure your mother can manage. It's just a wrist, not an arm or a leg. She has good friends and neighbours. They'll all help. Have you rung her? Did she say she wants you to go home?'

'Of course I haven't rung Mum, because she'd say to stay here. But I can't do that, not now that I know what's happened. She needs me, no matter what you think. And the salon needs me. They can't operate without two of their full-time hairdressers. We'll lose clients. Joanna said it was chaos there on Friday and Saturday. Fortunately, tomorrow is a slow day. By Tuesday, however, I'll have to be there.'

'Can't they find a temp?'

Her laugh was short and dry. 'When one of the girls went on maternity leave last year, we had the devil of a time finding someone to fill in for her. No way could we get someone on short notice. Look, there's no point arguing with me over this, John. My mind is made up. I've already rung the airline and got a seat on a flight leaving first thing in the morning. I have to be at the airport no later than six-thirty.'

'What? For pity's sake, Scarlet!' John exploded. 'This is ridiculous. Three more days up here. That's all you need. Three short days.

And you're going to throw it all away. Think of yourself for once. Your mother will survive. The business will survive. Okay, so you'll lose a bit of money and maybe a couple of clients. But you'll have what you've always wanted—a baby.'

One part of Scarlet—the selfish part—agreed with him. But she could not bear the thought of her mother struggling along at home without her. Neither could she let the girls in the salon down, not now that they'd asked for her help. On top of that, there was that other critical little matter of her having fallen in love with John.

This was her way out, Scarlet realised. Her escape clause. She would never have been able to walk away from him by herself, but she could do it for other people. Strange, how calm she felt about her decision. Maybe you were always calm when you knew you were doing the right thing.

'Even if I stayed here three more days, John, there's no guarantee of a baby.'

His eyes narrowed on her, his expression fierce. 'Why aren't you more upset about this?'

'I *am* upset about it.' God, did he honestly think she *wanted* to fall in love with him?

'No, you're bloody well not. You've grabbed onto this because you *want* to leave. You don't want me to be the father of your child. That's the bottom line, isn't it?'

She almost lied again. But what would have been the point?

'Yes,' she confessed. 'That's the bottom line.'

John could not believe how furious he was.

'So what did I do to change your mind?' he snapped.

'Nothing. The problem lies with me.'

'Meaning?'

Scarlet decided that a version of the truth would serve her purpose nicely. 'As unlikely as it seems, I'm in danger of becoming emotionally involved with you. It's a flaw in some women when they have great sex with a guy. But I don't want to fall for you, John. I really don't.'

'Why not?' he demanded to know, stung by her dismissive words.

She just stared at him, not believing that he could ask such a stupid question. 'Why do you think? You don't do love and marriage. You're a committed loner who only ever comes home at Christmas and has no concept of what it is to care about anyone but yourself. I don't believe you really want to be a father. I still can't fathom why you made your offer in the first place. It never did make sense to me.'

'Or to me,' he threw at her, his temper getting the better of him. 'It was an insanely impulsive gesture and one I regretted as soon as I made it. But then *you* contacted *me*, and I thought what the heck? Like I said, I'd always wanted you. And there you were, serving yourself up on a silver platter.'

Scarlet winced. She guessed she deserved that. But it hurt, oh so much. 'Charming,' she said, her chin lifting in defiance of her pain. 'It shouldn't bother you, then, if we call it quits at this stage. After all, you've already had me.'

'I sure have, sweetheart. I've already had everything I wanted from you!'

Tears threatened but she refused to cry in front of him. 'I always knew you were a bastard. I won't be cooking any of that fish. I couldn't eat a bite. I'll also be sleeping in the guest bedroom tonight.'

'Really? You don't want a goodbye session?'

She gave him a long, hard look, fully understanding how easily hate could become the other side of love. 'Don't bother driving me to the airport,' she bit out. 'I'll order a taxi.'

He almost called her back when she whirled to walk away. Almost told her…what?

That he was desperately sorry for what he had just said? That he hadn't meant *any* of it? That he *did* care? That he *did* want to be the father of her baby?

Let her go, his conscience insisted. *She's right. You're a selfish bastard. You'd make a rotten father. Even worse than your own. Go back over-*

seas somewhere. Africa, maybe. Get as far away from home—and Scarlet—as possible.

Yeah, that's what I'll do, John decided grimly. *As soon as possible.*

CHAPTER TWENTY-TWO

THE plane took off shortly after seven-thirty the following morning.

Scarlet leant back in her seat and closed her eyes. It had been a long night. She hadn't slept much, of course. Impossible in the face of such deep depression.

She'd rung her mother the previous evening at seven, as promised, immediately stating that she knew about her broken wrist and that she was coming home the following day. Her mother had argued with her but Scarlet had brooked no protest, glad finally to hear relief in her mother's voice. Relief and gratitude.

It had been hard, however, not breaking down during the call. She'd broken down afterwards, crying herself to sleep, a sleep which hadn't lasted long. She'd risen around midnight and crept out to the kitchen where she'd made herself some tea and toast. John hadn't stirred, thank heavens. Hadn't stirred the following morning, either. She'd crept out of the apartment down to the waiting taxi without having to face him again. Which was a relief. She couldn't have borne that.

Tears filled her eyes once more as she thought about their argument. He'd been so cruel. Yet there'd been truth in his words. She *had* contacted him. And she *had* enjoyed every moment of the sex, even before she'd fallen in love with him.

One thing falling in love with John proved, however: she had not been truly in love with Jason. If she had, she would have been devastated by his deception. But she hadn't been devastated, not the way she was devastated at this moment. Dear God, what was she going to do? She wasn't going to go back to that clinic, that was for sure. Not yet, anyway. She wasn't in a fit state to try that again, or even to contemplate becoming a single mother. A single mother had to be emotionally stable and strong. Had to be sure. Scarlet was no longer sure of anything. In truth, she was a mess.

The tears flooded in then, hot and strong. The poor lady sitting next to her became alarmed by her sobbing and called the steward, who brought her a box of tissues, followed by a brandy. She still cried on and off all the way back to Sydney but more quietly and discreetly.

By the time they landed, she'd run out of tears. The train trip back to Gosford was spent in a semi-comatose state. She rallied herself during the taxi ride home, determined not to do or say anything to make her mother suspicious. But it took a supreme effort of will to hide her distress behind a smile. Even worse was when her mother insisted on seeing all her photos, gushing over Darwin's natural beauty and declaring that one day they would both return to have a decent holiday there together.

The word 'decent' almost pushed Scarlet over the edge. Using exhaustion from the flight as an excuse, she hurried off to have a long, hot bath after which she forced herself to cook her mother dinner before retiring for the night. Fortunately, she slept like the dead, so she probably was exhausted, both physically and emotionally. The next morning she went into the salon early, making sure that by the time the other girls arrived everything was shipshape: the accounts. The orders. The equipment.

Everyone was thrilled to see her, Joanna especially.

'Your mum was annoyed with me for calling you,' Joanna told her privately. 'But I felt I had to.'

'You did the right thing, Joanna,' Scarlet said firmly and meant it.

It was difficult, however, to keep her mind on hairdressing that day. For some insane reason she kept hoping that John might contact her, either by phone or text. A silly hope, she realised by the end of the day. Why would he bother? It was over. They were over.

By Wednesday she was back on hairdressing autopilot, which was just as well, since she remained distracted. Her mum came into the salon with her, saying she could at least answer the phone and make coffee. Her wrist was in a cast but her fingers were operational and she was learning to use her left hand.

Scarlet was grateful for her company, especially during the tedious drive home at the end of the day. She'd distractedly taken the Central Coast highway instead of Terrigal Drive, and the traffic through the roadworks was worse, if that were possible. What a relief it would be when there were two lanes both ways instead of one. It should cut the bumper-to-bumper half-hour drive back to the ten minutes it should take from Erina to Terrigal. When she complained, her mother replied that at least it wasn't raining.

'You've brought the sunshine home with you,' she said, and smiled over at her daughter.

'If you say so, Mum,' Scarlet replied through gritted teeth.

Not that the sun was shining at that moment. It had already set a good fifteen minutes earlier.

Shortly after six, Scarlet turned into the road which led down to their street. She sighed as they rounded their corner, happy to be home. The sight of a strange silver car parked at the kerb outside their house brought a frown to her forehead. The car was very shiny and looked brand spanking new, not to mention expensive.

'Whose car's that, do you know?' she asked her mother as she swung into their driveway, barely five metres in front of the car, which she finally saw was a Lexus. So she'd been right about it being expensive. There was no one behind the wheel to recognise, but the car did carry New South Wales number plates plus the name of a Sydney dealership.

'I have no idea,' her mother replied. 'I doubt it's anyone for us.'

'True,' Scarlet said, pressing the remote which operated the garage door. She was sitting in her car, waiting whilst the garage door rolled its way slowly upwards, when something in her rear-vision mirror grabbed her attention. Swivelling her head around, she was utterly floored when she saw John walking across the road towards them, wearing an elegant grey suit with a shirt and tie. Her mouth literally dropped open as he came right up to her car and tapped on the passenger window.

'Goodness me!' her mother exclaimed. 'It's John Mitchell. Scarlet, wind my window down so that I can see what he wants.'

A wild mixture of emotions claimed Scarlet as she pressed the button which operated the window: shock. Confusion. Trepidation. But the strongest was a totally irrational joy.

'Yes, John, what is it?' her mother asked.

'Hi there, Mrs King,' he returned with a warm smile. 'Mum told me about your accident. I hope it's not causing you too much trouble.'

'I'm managing quite well, thank you, John. So what brings *you* home? I thought you'd gone back to Brazil.'

'That was my initial plan but something unforeseen happened and I've decided to come home to Terrigal to live. The thing is, Mrs King, I know Scarlet worked as an estate agent in this area for a good while and I was wondering if she might give me some advice on where and what to buy. I don't like to let grass grow under my feet so I was hoping to steal her away from you for a few hours tonight and get her advice over dinner. Mum said you're very welcome to have your dinner over at our place, so you won't have to worry about managing on your own. So what do you say, Scarlet?' he asked, glancing over at her with totally unreadable eyes. 'I have my own wheels this time,' he added, nodding towards the silver Lexus. 'You're not too tired, are you?'

What could she say when she was dying to find out what he was up to? Despite that burst of mad happiness at the sight of him, she could not believe that he seriously wanted to come back here to live. He would never do that. This was all just an excuse to get her alone. A ploy. A plan. John liked plans. But what plan was this?

A loud bell jangled in her head, warning her to be careful. Very careful.

'No, I'm not too tired,' she said, pleased that she sounded composed. 'But I would like to shower and change first. I've been at work all day. Give me half an hour, would you?'

'Fine. I'll be back, knocking on your front door, in half an hour.'

'Well that's a turn-up for the books,' Janet King said thoughtfully as she watched John retreat in the side-vision mirror. 'But not a total surprise. He always did fancy you, you know.'

'Oh, Mum, don't be ridiculous!' Scarlet said, scoffing, as she drove her car into the garage.

'I'm not being ridiculous. I have eyes. And you're not indifferent to him, either. I watched you both at Carolyn's fortieth. Play your cards right and you might not have to go back to that clinic.'

'Mum! I'm shocked.'

Her mother rolled her eyes at her. 'Scarlet King, you're thirty-four years old. Soon, you'll be thirty-five. We don't have time for shocked any more. Now what are you going to wear? Something sexy, I hope.'

Scarlet could not believe what she was hearing. She wanted to laugh at the irony of her mother virtually asking her to dress with the intention of seducing John. Little did the poor woman know that John was probably here on a mission to seduce *her*. It was the only thing which made sense. He hadn't liked it when she'd called it quits on him. He'd obviously come for more of what he'd had in Darwin.

At the same time, she could not deny that a small seed of hope had starting sprouting in her heart, no matter how illogical. This was another fatal flaw in women, Scarlet accepted wearily as she trudged from the garage to the house—their clinging to romance rather than reason. Hoping for a happily-ever-after ending as opposed to a more realistic one.

She didn't dress sexily. Her winter wardrobe wasn't sexy, though it was smart. She swiftly combined chocolate-brown wool trousers with a cream mohair jumper which had a wide boat neckline, trimmed with a row of chocolate-brown stitching. Her ankle boots were dark brown, her handbag fawn, made in imitation crocodile skin. She put her blonde hair up in a chic French roll, after which she remade her face before slipping elegant gold and pearl drops into her lobes. Lastly, she sprayed on some of her favourite perfume, which was vanilla based and not overpowering. She was just picking up the matching brown jacket from the bed when the front doorbell rang. A glance at her gold wristwatch showed John was a couple of minutes early.

Draping the jacket over her left arm—the night wasn't overly cold—she picked up her handbag and walked slowly from her room. Her mother had by then answered the door, calling out to Scarlet that she was leaving to go over to Carolyn's and not to forget her keys as she'd probably be asleep by the time John brought her home. By the time Scarlet reached the front hallway, her mother had disappeared across the road, leaving John standing under the porch light.

Scarlet was aware of her heart thudding behind her ribs as she walked towards him; aware, too, of his eyes on her, though they were annoyingly shadowed and still unreadable. Even when she drew close she was unable to discover anything from his expression. His face was as inscrutable as ever.

'I want to know why you're here,' she threw at him. 'No more lies now.'

'I haven't told any lies,' he replied with irritating composure.

'What?' she scoffed. 'I'm expected to believe you really mean to buy a house here in Terrigal?'

'Maybe not in Terrigal, but somewhere here on the Central Coast.'

'But you always said that…that…'

He stilled her stammering with a firm hand on her upper arm. 'Scarlet, do you think we could possibly have this conversation somewhere more private?'

'Oh,' she said weakly. 'Oh, okay.'

'Lock up, then, so that we can be on our way.'

She managed to lock up without dropping the set of keys. Just. John cupped her right elbow once she'd finished and steered her over to the passenger side of the Lexus. When he opened the door for her, she climbed in and belted up without speaking, possibly because she had no idea what to say. It wasn't often that Scarlet's mind resembled a tumble drier but this was one of those times.

'I've booked us a table at the Seasalt Restaurant in the Crowne Plaza,' John said as he climbed in behind the wheel. 'Mum assured me the food there is excellent. I've never been there for dinner myself. Actually, I haven't been anywhere local for dinner before. So this is a first for me in more ways than one,' he finished up as he started the car and drove off.

'Would you care to explain that remark?' Scarlet asked, having found her tongue at last.

'All in good time, Scarlet. All in good time.'

'I think now is as good a time as any,' she countered, unable to suppress her curiosity and her agitation any longer. 'We're alone. We're well away from our street now. For pity's sake, pull over and tell me what's going on.'

'Absolutely not. That's not how this is going to be done.'

'How *what* is going to be done?'

'I'm not going to have you tell our children in later years that their father proposed to you on the side of the road.'

'P-proposed?' Scarlet choked out, her eyes flinging wide as she stared over at him.

'You haven't heard of that word? And there I've been all these years, thinking you were highly intelligent. It means asking for your hand in marriage.'

Scarlet didn't know whether to laugh or cry. He couldn't be serious, could he?

Oh God, he *was*!

When a sob caught in her throat, he wrenched the car over to the side of the road, braking to a halt and snapping off the engine. 'Well, you've spoiled everything again now, haven't you? I was going to do this over a candlelit dinner with all the trimmings: music. Champagne. The works. But it seems some girls just can't wait.' As he turned to her he pulled a small silver box out of his jacket pocket and flipped the top open.

Another sob escaped Scarlet's lips when she saw what was nestled in a bed of dark blue velvet. Her hands came up to clasp her face, her happiness so great it was almost overwhelming.

'Oh, John,' she choked out.

'Scarlet King,' he said solemnly. 'I love you. No, that's understating things. I'm crazy about you and I simply can't live without you. Will you do me the honour of being my wife?'

Her eyes flooded, her heart too full for words.

His smile was gently wry. 'You once told me that the only use you had for a diamond was if it came atop a band of gold and with a proposal of marriage.'

Her smile, when it came, was full of a joy which had no bounds. It filled all those empty places in her heart and in her soul which had needed to be filled.

'It's so beautiful,' she murmured, reaching out to touch the huge solitaire diamond. 'Is it one of yours?'

'No. I actually don't have any truly decent diamonds in my gem collection. I bought this one yesterday in Sydney, along with this car and these clothes. I wanted to impress you.'

'I'm very impressed. But…'

'No buts. I know I told you once that I didn't do marriage; that I was a committed bachelor. But no man wants to remain a bachelor, Scarlet, once he truly falls in love. Trust me when I say all I want to do is spend every day of the rest of my life with you.'

'Oh dear,' she said, her heart having melted totally at his passionate declaration of love. Tears pricked at her eyes, tears of happiness.

'No don't say anything more till I've finished,' he raced on, perhaps worried that she was about to protest further. Which, of course, she was not.

'I dare say you're also concerned about my relationship with my family, especially my father. There's no need, Scarlet. Truly. I had a good long talk to Dad today and I found out something I wasn't aware of. Apparently, after Josh died, Dad went into a severe depression which was never properly treated. He only survived day to day by becoming a workaholic. It wasn't till he retired that Mum got him to see a more enlightened doctor and his condition was properly diagnosed and treated, which explains his change of mood lately. He told me today how sorry he was for the way he'd treated me, and Mum too. Terribly sorry.

'So you see, there's no reason for you to worry that I'm lying to you about coming to live near home. I'm actually looking forward it. I might even start up a local fishing-charter company rather than go back to mining work. After all, a family man shouldn't be travelling all over the place, doing dangerous things, should he?'

'Absolutely not,' Scarlet said, her voice thickening as her eyes welled up again.

'Hey, what's with all the tears? I thought you'd be happy.'

'I am happy. And, John…'

'Yes?'

'I love you too. Very much.'

His eyes gleamed. 'I sort of figured that out around the same time I figured myself out. Shortly after your plane took off. It just took me a while to work out what to do about it. I had to come up with a proper plan, you see.'

'Oh, you and your plans! I never did find out what your plan was for up in Darwin.'

'Mmm. Yes, well, that plan is still in operation.'

'Really? In what way?'

'I'll tell you all about it shortly. So is it a yes? Can I take the ring out of the box and slip it on your finger?'

She nodded and he did just that. It fitted her finger perfectly.

He clasped her hand tightly within both of his and looked deep into her eyes. 'I can't tell you how sorry I am for the dreadful things I said to you the other night, Scarlet. It was unforgiv—'

'Hush,' she broke in softly. 'Love is never having to say you're sorry.'

'Thank God for that,' he said with small laugh. 'Otherwise I could be apologising all night.'

'I'd rather have that candlelit dinner you told me about.'

'Me too.'

'There's only one small problem I can think of,' Scarlet said.

'What's that?'

'What on earth are we going to tell our families and friends? They're not going to believe in our engagement. It'll look much too sudden in their eyes.'

John frowned. 'You're probably right. You might have to hide that ring for a while, at least till you're safely pregnant.'

Scarlet's mouth dropped open whilst John just smiled. 'I did say that my Darwin plan is still in operation. It really was a good plan, involving great sex for days on end, followed by two or three days of abstinence till you entered your most likely to conceive phase…'

'Good grief!' Scarlet exclaimed.

'Yes, I know it sounds a bit much when you

say it out loud, but it's still a good plan. Given we've already been through an enforced abstinence phase, I didn't just book a table for dinner at the Crowne Plaza tonight. I booked us a room as well. And, before you say it, my darling wife-to-be, I know there are no guarantees of our making a baby tonight, but you have one thing going for you which is new—tonight, you will be made love to by a man who truly loves you. Tonight, you will feel safe and secure in his arms. Tonight, there will be no stress because, baby or not, we will still have each other till death do us part.'

Scarlet fought back more tears, having never been so moved in her life. She had read about the healing power of love but she'd never seen it for herself, or felt its power. But she felt it now and would never forget it.

'John Mitchell,' she choked out. 'They are the loveliest words I have ever heard. And you are the loveliest man. I think I must be luckiest girl in all the world to have found someone like you to love me.'

'I think I'm the lucky one here. But, before this deteriorates to a mutual admiration society, do you think we could move on? I haven't had a bite to eat in hours and I'm so hungry I could eat a whole barramundi all by myself!'

Scarlet smiled. She smiled on and off all night.

CHAPTER TWENTY-THREE

Fifteen months later

SCARLET tiptoed into the nursery and stood beside the rather large cot, her heart filling with joy and wonder as it always did when she looked down at her beautiful baby girls. It still amazed her to think that she and John had not made one baby that night, as they'd secretly hoped, but two.

Life had been kind to her for once. Very kind.

Any initial anxiety over expecting twins had soon been dispelled once she knew they were girls and, thankfully, not identical. John had claimed he wasn't worried at all, that he'd been thrilled to pieces by the news, but Scarlet had privately been of the opinion it wasn't a good idea to repeat a history which hadn't turned out well.

Jessica and Jennifer had been born a month early but so healthy that, after only a few days, their already besotted parents had been allowed to bring them home to the rather old but brilliantly located house which Scarlet had recommended John buy and which he had been spending all his time renovating and refurbishing. Situated between Wamberal and Terrigal beaches, it was only a short drive from both grandparents' homes, but far enough away to give them privacy. John hadn't bothered with his idea of a fishing-charter business as yet, saying he was too busy being a house husband. Not that Scarlet had returned to hairdressing. She hadn't. Looking after twins was a full-time occupation even with two doting grandmothers to help and a grandfather who, whilst not hands-on with the twins as yet—babies made him nervous—had become very hands-on helping John with the house. It made Scarlet happy to see that they were finally forging a good father and son relationship. A bit late perhaps, but better late than never.

A hand on her shoulder made her jump slightly.

'Your mum's here,' John said quietly as he bent to kiss her on the cheek. 'I told her the girls were sound asleep and to just sit down and watch TV whilst she could. Meanwhile, it's time we were off, madam. Although, before we go, can I just say how beautiful you look for an old married lady.'

'I do my best,' she said somewhat drily. Despite being madly in love, they hadn't given up their habit of verbal sparring.

'How long have we been married now? Oh yes. One year today. Twelve whole months. Three hundred and sixty-five days and you haven't divorced me yet. I think that deserves a reward, don't you?'

And there it was again, another silver box.

Scarlet's heart squeezed tight when he flipped it open. This time, it wasn't a diamond which graced the band of gold but three different stones: an emerald in the middle flanked by a sapphire and a ruby, the design curved so it sat perfectly against the large diamond solitaire of her engagement ring.

'Now these *are* from my personal gem collection,' John said as he slipped the eternity ring on her finger.

'It's a truly beautiful ring and I love it. But, John, I really didn't expect you to get me anything else. You've already filled the living room with flowers.'

'Which is exactly why you deserve more. Because you didn't expect it. Any other wife would have.'

'You're in danger of spoiling me.'

'True. But what else have I got to do with my money?'

'Yes, I can see that. But money doesn't buy happiness, John. Happiness is what we have here, in this cot. It comes from love and family. Which is why my anniversary present to you is something I can't wrap up in a box.'

'Fess up, woman. What have you done?'

'We're not just going to the Crowne Plaza for an anniversary dinner tonight. I've booked us a room.'

'But...'

'No buts, John. Mum's staying the night with our babies and we're staying the night in the honeymoon suite.'

'The honeymoon suite!'

Her shrug was carefree. 'Money doesn't buy you happiness, John, but it does buy you the opportunity for pleasure. If you recall, we haven't had any sex for at least a week.'

'Mmm. Yes. I did notice. You said you were too tired every night.'

'I lied. I was just making sure you'd be totally unable to resist me tonight.'

He shook his head at her. 'You are a devious woman.'

'And you are a magnificent lover.'

'Flattery won't get you anywhere.'

'That's what I thought. So, just to make sure, I left off my underwear.'

He stared at her, then smiled a wicked smile.
'You do realise I'll make you have dinner first.'
She smiled. 'Want to bet on that?'
He grinned. 'But of course.'
He won.

Nine months later a boy was born. They called
him Harry, after John's grandfather.

* * * * *